Her Second-Chance Hero

LINDA BARRETT

DEDICATION

To David –

As a boy, you made me laugh

As a man, you've made me proud.

Love, Mom

Cover art by Rogenna Brewer

www.sweettoheat.blogspot.com

E-book and print formatting by Web Crafters

www.webcraftersdesign.com

Copy Editing by Amy Knupp

www.blueotterediting.com

CHAPTER ONE

Red Sox Training Camp, Ft. Myers, FL
April 2012

His D-Day had arrived.

Mike Romano's shoulder ached with every pitch. Standing on the mound, he glanced left then right, buying time before hurling the next ball. He knew how to hide pain. Every player did, at least for awhile. Now he needed to wear a cop face like Chief O'Brien's from Pilgrim Cove, Mike's hometown. That man knew how to scare a teenager. He borrowed O'Brien's mask and wound up again.

Releasing the next pitch, he bit his lip. The team manager, doctor, and catcher watched his every move while a few hitters stood ready to bat against him. The empty stadium felt weird. Mike wished the seats held a slew of fans to energize him.

After he'd spent three years in the organization's minor league, moving up to the majors had been the turning point he'd worked toward every single day. And two years ago, Mike's efforts had paid off. He'd gotten in one full season of elite play. One full season on the starting roster of the Boston Red Sox. Mike had achieved the dream of almost every little boy in America. One of the few who made it.

And then a rotator cuff injury, the bane of all pitchers, had put him on the inactive list in post-season play. Surgery and a year of physical therapy hadn't provided the magic. Mike knew it—he felt it—each time he threw the ball. With a glance at the blank faces of those in the stadium, Mike knew something else. They were going to cut him from the team.

His dream career was over before catching fire. His chest tightened as he walked toward the officials, but he managed to produce a weak smile. And then it was done. Except for the phone call to come.

Less than an hour later, he put personal stuff in his car and hit a familiar number on his cell.

"Dad?"

"Mike! How's my favorite son?"

An old joke. Mike was Paul Romano's only son, only child. He swallowed hard. They'd shared the dream, and his dad would be disappointed.

"Not so good. Is my old room still available for a while? Seems like I'm a has-been at the ripe old age of twenty-eight."

Silence. "You get up here as soon as possible. You can help me in the business until you figure things out. And I know you will."

Mike had never had a Plan B, and he wasn't sure about how to "figure things out." It seemed, however, that his dad had enough confidence for both of them.

Pilgrim Cove, eight months later
December 2012

The threat of snow and his flaring arthritis didn't stop Bart Quinn from bringing a huge welcome basket from Quinn Realty and Property Management to Alison Berg-Martin, the newest permanent resident of Pilgrim Cove. His partner and granddaughter, Lila, had worked closely with him to find the perfect rent-to-buy property.

The young widow from Boston, had given them a punch list of criteria, beginning with safety. No house with beach or bay access. Her baby son had started walking and would want to explore. Bodies of water were too dangerous. Much too dangerous. As were busy streets and cars. Could he find a quiet area? He and Lila had done their best, but the more private, the more expensive. Alison couldn't afford that luxury, not while living on a death benefit from her husband and small trust from her grandfather.

Bart exited his reliable old Town Car, reached for the gift, and waited for Lila to join him from her own vehicle.

"Glad you're with me, today," he said as they walked toward the second house from the corner of Neptune Street. "Alison needs to make friends her own age."

"Maybe. But don't push her, Granddad. She needs to find her way."

"I never push, darling. I just…uh…"

"Manipulate? Arrange? I love you dearly, but I've been around you a long time and know exactly how you work."

Bart chuckled. His lassie was right. Normally he manipulated the young people living in Sea View House, but he'd walked softly with this young woman. Alison had stayed there only a month last June with her infant

3

boy before deciding to relocate permanently. He glanced from Alison's new house to where the Romanos lived across the street. Father and son together full-time as of eight months ago. A disappointment for the boy, to be sure. But just perfect now. Mike Romano would be exactly what Alison Berg-Martin needed...in just a little more time.

He and Lila rang the bell.

At the sound of the doorbell, one-year-old Joey crawled faster than Alison walked, despite the cartons and boxes littering the floor. She ran to her son, scooped him up, and grabbed a light blanket. "Peek-a-boo," she crooned while draping it over him. She had to protect him from the cold, especially his head. Wasn't that in the baby books?

When she spotted Bart and Lila through the sidelight, she opened the door and smiled. "Welcome to my mess."

"We won't stay but a minute," said Lila, closing the door behind her. "Just wanted to bring some sunshine on a gray winter day." She took the basket from Bart but addressed Alison. "Your arms are full. Where...?"

"The dining room table should do it. It's a beautiful bouquet. Thank you."

"Welcome to Pilgrim Cove," said Bart. "Now let's see who's hiding under that blanket." He pulled the covering off. "Peek-a-boo!"

The child squealed with excitement and bounced in his mother's arms.

"He's adorable," said Lila, "and look at that hair! Like a copper penny." A smile grew as she glanced at Alison. "Mother and son are unmistakable."

"You should have seen his father," said Alison. "Spitting image except for the hair." She'd heard the hair comparison often. Redheads were the rare breed, and

Joey and she were a match. But that left Peter out of the conversation. *Oh, Peter. You are missing so much.*

She blinked away tears that still came too easily. Not even unexpected guests could distract her enough. She tried to smile, however, as she led them farther inside.

"Thank you very much. Not only flowers but cookies, candy…" The basket held a full array of temptation.

"A small token to say you're not alone," said Bart. "New to town? Aye. But you've got friends, lassie. Right here."

The man reminded Alison of her dad. He also reminded her of Peter. Big men. Blustering men. Loving hard and spewing reassurances as if they could protect all in their care. But who protected them?

"I'll be fine as long as Joey is happy. And safe." She kissed the baby on the cheek and bounced him in her arms. "No more big cities. Ever again."

The ensuing silence was broken by Lila. "I grew up in Pilgrim Cove, fell in love here, and suffered heartache here, too. But it worked out." She patted her stomach. "You can't tell much yet, but Jason and I are expecting our second at the end of May."

"It's the magic," said Bart. "And you've been sprinkled with it, too, lass. You stayed in Sea View House last June and came back to stay for good."

Magic? More like black magic. Mr. Quinn was quite the character.

"Granddad, enough drama!" Lila rolled her eyes. "What I'm trying to say, Alison, is that we're a good town, but we're not Shangri-La. We're real people. Just like anywhere else."

Alison had liked Lila Parker from the beginning of the house-hunting experience. Open and honest. Maybe they'd become real friends. "I've done my research," she said. "Crime is low here. Schools are good. Joey's grandparents are all in Boston, which is a manageable ride, and that's good enough for me."

"Ah, then they'll be sure to come down for Christmas," said Bart.

Without Peter? No. No holidays this year. No Christmas. No Hanukkah. No nothing. But her decision was nobody's business. She shrugged. "We'll see."

"The ROMEOs are all in town," said Bart, extracting a business card from his inside coat pocket. "No snowbirds running south for the winter. So if you need anything at all, have questions, want a referral…you can count on us. We know everyone."

Alison took the card listing Bart's buddies, all Retired Old Men Eating Out, with phone numbers and specialties. "If I need an electrician, I'll call Ralph Bigelow. But right now, I need a pediatrician, and I don't think the ROMEOs have the answer!"

"But I do," said Lila. "Actually Doc Rosen, who's on that list, recommended her years ago, and we've all been very happy, including my ten-year-old daughter, Katie." She scrambled through her purse for pencil and paper. "Here you go." Turning toward the door, she said, "And now we'll leave you to unpack in peace."

Alison sensed the instant Lila spotted the cello case lying on its side. Saw the interest illuminating the woman's face. Knew she'd be asking questions, and her own stomach tensed. She had to cut the conversation off before it began.

"I haven't played it in a very long time." With a casual wave of her hand, she added, "Maybe I'll give it away."

As if. The instrument had been a gift. A three-hundred-year-old Italian-crafted gift worth more than the house she'd just leased. She hoped, however, that she'd diminished Lila's enthusiasm.

"Wow. If you really mean that, please keep me in mind. The kids in my family are incredibly talented. Another instrument would be a happy challenge for them." She stepped closer and grinned. "As my husband learned—the hard way, of course—and now says, 'talent is not to be trifled with. Nurture the gift. '"

Alison shivered from head to fingertips to toes. Echoes from the past. *Nurture the gift.* Lila's husband must be the real deal. Her mind raced through the Boston area musicians she knew, relieved not to recognize the name Parker. She was starting a new life. "I-I'm sorry…?"

"Jason. Jason Parker."

It took a moment before the aha. Lila's husband was definitely the real deal. At the top of the pop charts—composer, singer, performer. A piano man. Thank God their lives wouldn't cross musically. Maybe she'd rethink a friendship with Lila.

The bell rang just as Alison and her guests reached the door. She pulled it open, looked up, a long way up past the scruffy beard, and stared into the bluest eyes she'd ever seen.

"Mike Romano," he said, thrusting a package at her, "from across the street." A delicious aroma emanated from the bag. "It's shepherd pie. My dad likes to cook, and you probably need some supper." He stared at her, then glanced at the others. "The snow's started, and we're going to have some wicked weather. You'd better get on home. Want me to drive you, Bart?"

The older man glared. "Ask me again in twenty years, boy-o."

Romano smiled, a sweet, crooked, one-side-of-his-mouth smile, and a corner of Alison's heart tore. So familiar.

"Thank you, and thank your dad," she said, now watching her other guests walk to their vehicles.

7

Romano hadn't lied. The snow was starting to fall in serious fashion.

"Here's my business card, Red. The home number's on it. If you lose electricity in the storm or need anything, give us a call."

Joey had fallen asleep in her arms, and she gave him a kiss. "I've got to put him down. He's getting heavier every day." She placed the baby carefully in his porta-crib and once more turned to her neighbor.

"My name's Alison. Don't call me Red or Lucy or carrottop."

Mike Romano's attention traveled from the baby to her. "My hearing's not too good, Red. But I come in handy from time to time."

If he was trying to be funny, he'd failed. "I'm not laughing, Mr. Romano." She looked at his card. *Romano Landscape and Design.* "Nice. So are you on vacation all winter?"

That crooked grin appeared again. "I manage to keep busy. Street plowing…firefighting…planning landscape designs for spring installation. We cut and trim trees for the county to keep the roads safe. No time to loiter."

Impressive. "Sounds like you handle everything but the kitchen sink."

He winked. "For that you call a plumber."

She burst out laughing. It was the weirdest thing, the juxtaposition of her and the baby in a god-awful messy house, talking with a bunch of strangers, and a guy calling her Red. Nothing made sense. Especially her giggles.

Nerves. Stress. Relieved by a lame joke. Mike Romano's stupid joke.

"I think you've broken the spell," she gasped. "I haven't laughed since my husband died."

He rubbed the back of his neck. "Yeah. I-I'm very sorry for your loss. But not for the laughter. They say it's the best medicine."

"A cliché, but maybe…" She shrugged.

Mike scanned the house, left and right and behind Alison. "Looks like you've got a load of work ahead. So I'll let you at it." He opened the door, then paused. "Got my number, just in case?"

Oh, she had his number. A born flirt with a sense of humor hard to ignore. Probably picked up women wherever he went. At least she didn't have to deal with that. She held up his business card. "Got it."

He waved and left.

She glanced at her son, then at the door. "He couldn't get away fast enough." Shrugging, she made her way to the kitchen and began to unpack.

Mr. Blue Eyes didn't matter. Her music didn't matter. Against the advice of her symphony friends and Maestro Bekker, she'd resigned her second-chair cello position from the South Shore Philharmonic.

Nothing mattered to her anymore. Except little Joey.

CHAPTER TWO

Six months later—June 2013

Mike Romano swept his gaze over the landscape design his crew had implemented at Sea View House that day and nodded in approval. The large rhododendrons with their purple blossoms broke up the monotony of the siding, softening the image of the large two-family home. His men had planted a variety of annuals—petunias, zinnias, Vinca—to provide the "facelift" Bart Quinn had wanted, and whatever Quinn wanted, Quinn got. The old curmudgeon had full control of the property and paid his bills on time. Mike's gardeners had mowed, edged, and fertilized the lawn. Everything looked great for Rebecca Hart, the current temporary tenant.

He sighed in sympathy. Poor woman. Losing a leg in the Boston Marathon bombing two months ago. Well, that qualified her as a special person, worthy of Sea View House. He walked down the driveway to the back door, knocked, and waited.

When Rebecca opened the door, she stood balanced with crutches, perspiration running down her temples. "Sorry I'm such a sweat hog," she said with a grin, "but I had to do my physical therapy."

He winced in sympathy. Special exercises hadn't worked for him, but he wasn't going to burst her bubble.

"Good for you." He pointed toward the street. "We're done in front. Hope you enjoy the yard. We'll be mowing every week."

"Great. And thanks. I truly love being surrounded by the outdoors, whether ocean views or uplifting gardens. Colorful flowers and plants are good for the soul."

He stood quietly. "That's food for thought."

Returning to his truck, he thought of another lady, closer to home, whose soul needed some feeding. Alison Berg-Martin. But maybe that wasn't his job. They didn't get along very well. Sure, she was polite. But if he hadn't seen her laughing with and cuddling her son, he would have written her off as an ice queen. At least with him.

He drove across town to Bay Road and pulled into the employee lot of the garden center. Even at the end of the day, the customer side was half-full. He spotted his dad out back, walking through tables of plants and talking to people, gesturing, explaining. Animated. Paul Romano loved his business and had welcomed Mike back last year.

"It's a family business," his dad had insisted. "It's always been a family business."

But it hadn't been Mike's first choice.

Mike had chuckled and shook his head. "Let's be honest, Dad. I may have worked alongside you as a kid, but my head was elsewhere."

"I know, I know." He'd slapped Mike on the back. "But it'll work out."

11

Now Mike scanned the scene. Sophie was at Paul's side. Their yellow lab had become a fixture in the place, and more than earned her keep. Her job? Sophie was the ambassador of friendliness, who kept the kids entertained so parents could browse in peace for whatever they needed—shrubs, trees, flowers, and a myriad of other garden-related items. Some of the regulars came with treats.

Mike waved to his dad and dog, and gestured toward their private office. Payables, receivables, plant deliveries, customer appointments—residential and commercial—the landscape business required the same attention as any other business. Of course, few other enterprises produced the kind of aesthetics that they did. "Good for the soul," he murmured while he headed to his desk, prepared to keep his eye on the ball—this time, the bottom line. His heart wasn't in it, but for his dad's sake, he'd carry on.

Good for the soul... Dang! His pretty little neighbor and her baby boy couldn't go on forever living in isolation. If Rebecca Hart could come back swinging after the marathon bombing, so could Red. He was going to crack that ice. He looked outside. Still had a bunch of daylight left. He'd go straight home tonight instead of stopping for a brewski with the guys.

From her seat on the front porch, Alison heard the engine before she saw the motorcycle and its rider. The bike made an awful noise, a disturbing-the-peace kind of noise. She could track her neighbor's comings and goings based on the sound. At this time of the evening— a beautiful evening—she knew Mike Romano was home from work.

"Big deal," she said to Joey, inserting a spoonful of mashed carrots into his mouth and glad for the large bib. The baby was strapped into his stroller. Alison had learned the hard way not to underestimate her 18 month old son. Joey moved at lightning speed, and safety straps were in order. She glanced at the large carton on the floor. Installing a wide gate at the top of the steps was her next project. The instructions didn't seem too difficult. She'd tackle it after Joey was asleep for the night.

"Hey, Red." The man was coming up her walk.

She glared. "I'm ignoring you."

"You can try, but he's not."

Joey bounced in the carriage, shrieking in excitement. "Up, up." He held out his arms to Mike. "Man, man."

"Hey, buddy. Your vocabulary's improving." Mike stooped down beside the boy. "Time to eat your dinner."

A stream of Joey's animated gibberish, meaningful only to him, followed with Mike commenting from time to time. "He's a great conversationalist," he said, smiling at Alison.

And once more, Michael Romano managed to worm his way around her, easing her annoyance. She blamed the tilted smile.

"So why are you hanging around tonight, Romeo...uh, I mean Romano? No date?"

He sat back on the floor, his brows drawing together. "Huh?"

"Come on. Don't play the innocent. A different woman every week is what I hear. And tonight's Friday, the biggest date night...."

"Which must mean I'm losing my touch. Forget every *week*. In the old days, I saw a different girl every *night*. So put that in your pipe..."

She put her hand up. "Uncle. I'm crying uncle."

His blue eyes widened. "Oh, no, you're not. You're not a quitter. You're just getting ready for the next round."

And suddenly, tears gathered. She swallowed hard. Who knew that an unexpected splash of humor could tear her apart? The man didn't even know what he was saying.

"Hey, Alison. What did I do?"

She shook her head. "Every day is the 'next round. ' It's hard."

"But little Joey is worth it. Right?"

"What kind of a dumb question is that? Of course he is." She leaned into the stroller and nuzzled the baby. "I love you so much, Joey boy." And got a cheek covered with saliva kisses.

Mike cleared his throat. "Not that I have personal experience," he began, speaking slowly, "but it seems to me that being a single parent is very hard. And you're doing great."

She shrugged. "Great? We'll know in twenty years. For right now, I suppose I'm doing the best I can." The light was fading. "Want to finish feeding him so I can install that gate?" She pointed to the carton.

Mike's glance wavered between the carriage and the box. "Nope. You feed; I'll handle the gate."

"Figures. Traditional division of labor." But she smiled. At this point, she wouldn't turn down any offer of help with chores. "Thank you very much."

##

Her sweet smile hit him in waves. Brown eyes, warm and crinkling at the corners, shining a happy light. Her skin, blushing the light pink of Leonardo da Vinci roses. And her mouth with its dimple on the side—so cute. Not to mention a chin that seemed to challenge him.

Had he been blind all winter? Or afraid?

Too late now. The undertow she exerted tugged at him, threatening to drag him down. He tensed and jumped to his feet, ready to run. He liked to keep things simple, and all he saw were complications. Trouble.

But her smile remained as she glanced toward the carton. Right. The safety gate. He pulled out a ring of keys, where he kept his Swiss Army knife. Always handy.

"Good," he said, reading the label. "You chose one of my suppliers."

"Did I?"

"Yeah, but I could have gotten you a better price." He cut the sealing tape.

"I'll remember next time."

"And another thing…your landscaping sucks. I'm going to create something new for the front of the house. Maybe flowering shrubs against the fence. Definitely clusters of color in the beds." He focused on his chore, bracing for her reaction, and didn't have long to wait.

"Oh, no, you're not. That's much too expensive. I'll get to it myself eventually."

"I give a big discount to friends." If a garden helped Rebecca at Sea View House, it would be good for Alison, too. Upheavals took many forms. So did healing. He'd been learning about adjusting expectations after being dropped from the Sox. It seemed some injuries never healed quite enough. Some dreams never died, and some decisions haunted forever.

"You'll starve if you give out big discounts," said Alison. "And all that work would take you away from better paying customers."

He removed the gate from the carton and plastic wrap and expanded it from post to post across the top of the steps. Well made, easy to install. Perfect.

"You made a good choice." He began connecting the ends to the posts.

"You already said that. And you didn't answer my questions."

He'd give her a half truth. He pointed to his house across the street. "When I come out the door every day, I see your yard, and it hurts my eyes. So I'm designing it for me!"

She chuckled and reached for her son, freeing him from the carriage and standing him on the ground. "Liar, liar, pants on fire," she said, looking at Mike. "You don't strike me as being *that* sensitive."

Joey found his balance and took off down the porch. Walking was not in his repertoire.

"If you watch him for a minute, I'll get some toys." Alison disappeared into the house before he could reply.

Joey seemed to like his freedom. Running, running until he fell. Right on his rump. The surprise on his face was comical. But then the clouds formed, and Mike knew a screech wasn't far behind.

"Hey, Joey. Over here."

The baby turned on his hands and knees. Mike squatted a distance away. "Man, man." He speed-crawled to Mike and babbled again in that language only another toddler could understand. Until he said, "Up. Man. Up." And raised his hands.

"All right, kiddo. Let's walk." He placed Joey on his feet, took his hand, and jogged the length of the porch together. "Good job, buddy. Give me five!"

He showed Joey the iconic motion of congratulations. They slapped hands again. And again. A new game. "What's taking Mommy so long?"

"Mommy's right here."

But her laughter had gone, the gleaming eyes now shadowed, and Mike knew Alison's mind was somewhere else. He wondered how long she'd been watching them.

"Snap out of it, Red. You've got an audience." He nodded at her son.

She pivoted toward him so hard he thought she'd fall over. "Don't give me orders. I'm doing the best I can." She snatched Joey to her, nuzzled him, but spoke to Mike. "Don't you have a date or something? Somewhere else to go?"

"So you can hide in the house alone and cry all night?"

Her eyes couldn't get any wider. Her mouth formed a perfect circle, but the rapid rise and fall of her chest was the giveaway. He heard her gasping breaths, and yet, she remained silent. Until… "You…you have no right to speak to me like that. No right at all. Who do you think you are?"

"Then tell me I'm wrong, that you weren't planning to hide away in a corner. Tell me instead"—he aimed for the jugular now, each word deliberate—"that you were going to play the cello, reclaim your life, and find some comfort."

The door slammed in his face with enough force to make the neighbors wonder.

"I'll be back in the morning, Red," he called out. "Early."

How did he know about her cello? She'd never spoken to anyone about it, about her wonderful tenure with the South Shore Philharmonic. More important, how could he know how the sounds of the instrument could fill her heart, her soul? He spoke of comfort. An understatement. When she played, she soared somewhere else, somewhere magical. More than comfort, it was heaven. A heaven she tried to share with the audience. *Come with me. Dream with me. Fly with me. Empty yourselves of everything but the music.*

But that was then…

And while she had flown, Peter had fallen. A drug bust. Part of the job she'd tried to ignore…except that time she couldn't. That time Pete had been the "officer down." A horrible phrase. She'd imagined the scene a thousand times and wished she could change the ending. The reality, however, was the presence of Pete's brothers-in-blue when she'd walked through the backstage exit of the Boston concert hall, so eager to see Peter, to finally share the wonderful news of their pregnancy. One look at his friends—their posture, their faces—and she'd known the truth.

She groaned in memory, her guilt piercing her. Her loving husband never knew he was to become a dad. She'd waited too long to share the good news.

He may have died a hero in the eyes of the world, but he'd been her own personal hero, too. When he'd come along, she'd known he was special. She sighed a deep sigh and began humming the melody to Mariah Carey's "Hero," a song that seemed to haunt her.

"Ready for a bath, sweetheart?" Her job now was to raise their son. "Daddy was a hero, but you're not going to be a cop when you grow up." She blew raspberries on his naked tummy. "Get it?"

Gurgles and laughter, a bath, a bottle. A rocking chair. Only at night did Joey take the bottle, and she'd postponed weaning him off it—for her sake, if not his. A quiet time, private and relaxed. Another day of growing for Joey, another day of trying for her.

Joey's arm waved in the air. He grabbed her hand, hit it with his palm, and turned from the bottle. "Fi.

Man. Gi me five!" He sighed and latched on to the nipple again. His lids closed, sucking slowed, and breathing became rhythmic and steady. Down and out.

Alison placed him in his crib, made sure the monitor was on, and returned downstairs. *Give me five?* She walked to the front of the house and glanced through the window. The motorcycle was gone. Well, what did she expect? It was a gorgeous Friday night. The most eligible bachelor in Pilgrim Cove wouldn't waste it.

In the kitchen, she filled the kettle and placed it on the stove. Maybe chamomile tea tonight—it was supposed to help with sleeping. Just like listening to classical music had helped Pete fall asleep at home or at a concert. She chuckled at the memory. He'd been her most ardent admirer, offering unwavering support and the kind of confidence she'd wished she'd been born with.

Confidence. Her neighbor had it, too. In spades. Two strong men. She must attract them. So what did that mean? That she projected weakness? An old-fashioned damsel in distress?

She didn't think so. She'd had the chutzpah to make her own way in a competitive career. To win blind auditions and play solo before thousands. A scaredy-cat wouldn't do that. But being a mom scared her. The loving came easy, but the doing…? Doing things right?

With her cup of tea next to her, she sat at the table and booted up her laptop. Email first. Her folks wanted to visit. Her in-laws wanted to visit. She opened the calendar and made some notes. Seemed like the following weekends would be booked.

Her friend, violinist Karen Gallagher, was checking in. Catching up. Was Alison playing again? Was she ever coming back to Beantown? Alison sighed and replied, inviting Karen to the beach.

She checked baby and childcare websites. Took notes about eighteen-month-olds and the expectations for normal growth. She had a library of childcare books, but the latest information from medical journals and popular magazines were online. After searching for the Pilgrim Cove site, she checked the library's summertime story hours. She wished they offered a parenting class.

In a light bulb moment, she solved the mystery of how Mike Romano knew about her cello and career. The Internet. He must have looked her up online. With shaking hands, she went onto the Philharmonic's website, and dang! There she was. Alison Berg. They had her picture, a profile, and listed as taking a leave of absence. Not true! She had resigned. She tapped a few more keys and opened her own personal website, which displayed her picture, bio, and accomplishments. She'd forgotten about the website, but now she'd have it taken down. It was time to disappear from the music world.

CHAPTER THREE

Crunch. Tap. Crunch, tap.

Early the next morning, before Joey had made a sound, Alison heard an unfamiliar clatter of activity coming from her front yard. She put on her cotton robe, went downstairs, and looked out the window.

Mike Romano. And Sophie. The man wore a sweatband around his forehead, tee shirt, jeans, work boots, and held a shovel in his gloved hands. A wheelbarrow stood close to him. A row of little flags were aligned in a curved arc on the ground on either side of the porch. While the dog relaxed in the morning sun, Mike dug the area inside the flags, scooping out sections of grass and placing them in the wheelbarrow. Probably for later use. Alison knew her new landscaping would have a generous amount of plants and flowers. But the work! Mike's skin shone with his effort, his hands around the shovel, arms flexing as he dug.

She stared transfixed as the tight tee shirt outlined the man's every muscle. Her breath hitched and a shiver flew through her body. Something was wrong with her.

Twirling from the window, she went to the kitchen and put up a pot of coffee—the least she could do.

She stepped outside. "You started early."

With the shovel, he lifted another section of grass and placed it on top of the pile he'd started. Then he looked at Alison, his dark eyes gleaming. "Good morning."

A killer smile.

"Morning." She walked closer. "I was surprised to see you with the sunrise."

"Huh?"

"You took off shortly after you left here last night. I heard the engine."

"And…?"

She shrugged, suddenly uncomfortable. "Well, yesterday was Friday, and I thought…you'd be out late."

He didn't respond immediately but a moment later emitted a hard laugh. "You thought I'd be with six different women having a wild time?" He shrugged, shot a hard glance at her, but spoke softly as he answered his own question. "Maybe I was. Maybe I wasn't."

And maybe she'd keep her mouth shut next time. Not her business. "Coffee's ready. I'll be right back."

"I take it black. Thanks."

A minute later, Alison watched him raise his cup. "Here's to you, Red. To your new life in Pilgrim Cove."

She tried to smile. "Not that I wanted a new life…."

His eyes darkened as he stared at her. "Yeah, I know. You never see it coming." He grunted. "I guess the gotcha about living—about life—is that it happens on an ever-changing field of dreams."

##

Each morning during the next week, Alison stepped outside with two cups of coffee, marveling at the progress Mike had made in her yard. Evidently his private life did not interfere with his self-appointed task. A garden was taking shape before her eyes.

"We're anchoring the yard with hydrangeas on each side of the stairs. You'll have big white flowers from now until autumn. And for contrast, roses next to them—a lady has to have pink roses...."

She watched an artist at work and wondered if baseball had been an art for him, too. At the end of the week, clouds of color enlivened her front yard. Pinks, lavender, corals. And for fun, black-eyed Susans and day lilies had their space, hardy for New England and perennials. She'd enjoy them for years to come. Mike had transformed a swath of plain green grass into a delightful garden. As a bonus, some plants attracted butterflies. She'd have to think of something to repay him.

He was finishing his daily stint on Saturday morning when her parents pulled up.

Her mom hugged and kissed her, and held her at arm's length for a better examination. "Hmm. Better. Looking better." She waved at the garden. "And if this is a reason, then it's wonderful. You've got something going on here." She nodded at Mike. Petted Sophie. "Great job. I love gardens." Turning back to Alison, she said, "Now where's the baby?"

"Nice to see you, too," Alison joked. "He's not quite up yet, but...go on in."

She stepped toward the tall, quiet man who patiently waited. "Hi, Dad." Wrapped in his arms, she felt herself relax. He cupped her face in his hands. "How are you, sweetheart?"

"Fine. I get through the day. Joey keeps me busy."

"Of course. But..."

"I'm trying, Dad."

"Ahem," came a familiar voice. "No, she's not."

To her disbelief, Mike approached, arm extended, and shook hands with her father. "Mike Romano." He nodded toward his house. "I live there with my dad and Sophie, here, and met your daughter on the day she moved in. So I speak the truth."

"This is a private conversation, Mr. Romano." She pointed across the street. "Don't you have a business to run?"

"Don't you have a cello to play?"

Shocked, she couldn't speak for a moment, but flung her arm wide. "Get out. And don't come back. I'll finish the yard myself."

His laughter surprised her. "You're not scaring me, Red. In fact, you're cute when you're mad. So let me make you a little angrier. Have you cleaned the strings and fingerboard in the last six months? Did you use a humidifier this winter to prevent cracking and warping? Did you rosin your bow?"

"For crying out loud…" Where was he coming from?

He reached out and gently pushed her chin up. "You can close your mouth now. When I wasn't playing baseball, I played bass and percussion in the high school jazz band. Not up to your standards, I'm sure, but plenty of fun. And I learned a lot."

Mike nodded at Alison's dad. "Have a great visit. Sorry if my comments aren't welcome, but they're warranted. And I need an ally."

David Berg's eyebrows rose.

"Come on inside, Dad. Mike likes to butt into everything."

"But is he right, honey? That's the real question."

She paused and looked from one man to the other. "There are no rules about grief. Everyone goes at her own pace, including me. The subject is now closed…except…" She deliberately paced toward Mike.

"Of course I took care of the cello," she said, poking him in the chest. "It was a gift. And it's beautiful, valuable, and it's-it's mine!"

"'Atta girl," cheered her dad.

"Exactly." Mike waved and headed home.

##

Alison and her family headed to the beach after breakfast, before the sun became too strong. She wanted Joey's first venture there to be without mishap. She packed the car with everything but the kitchen sink, as her mom said.

"We're only a few blocks away," said Carol. "Let's put what we need in the stroller and walk."

But Alison wanted the Pak 'n Play and the large beach umbrella, not to mention all the toiletries and toys a baby might require.

"How do you do this when we're not here?" asked her mother. "You can't handle all this stuff yourself and keep your eye on Joey, too."

Alison shrugged. "I don't go during the week."

"But-but you live at the beach!" Her mom's eyes widened; her brows rose. "I thought you wanted to immerse yourself in the whole scene—ocean, sand, big sky. Something different. Something…comforting."

Alison bit her lip. After six months, *she* didn't feel any different than she had in the city. But she didn't feel any worse, either.

"Joey is better off here," she said. "I love the house, and I'll buy it as soon as I can afford it. I'm not moving back."

"You'll need a job to qualify for a mortgage."

"I know." But she couldn't think about a job yet. Too complicated.

She pulled into a spot at the corner of Beach Street and Outlook Drive, right near a big gray house, then placed her parking permit on the dashboard. "Residents only," she explained. "Parking's tough in season."

"Just look at that garden," said Carol, getting out of the car and pointing at the house's front yard. "As beautiful as yours. Clouds of color in front of the spiky hostas. Those are impatiens and lilies, and just look at that clematis vine around the lamppost. It's going to be beautiful in time."

"That's Sea View House," said Alison, lifting Joey from his car seat and handing him to his grandma. "It's where Joey and I stayed last June, when I first came to Pilgrim Cove. It's rumored to be a special place. Bart Quinn thinks magic infuses the house. He even wanted me to rent it again for a season before doing the rent-to-buy deal, but I laughed. The only magic I'd believe in is going back in time and seeing Peter again. But no house could perform that kind of miracle."

Her mom's worried gaze went from her to her dad and back to her. "One thing's for sure. We do need a miracle...not for Peter, not for Joey, but for you, Alison. For you."

Her mouth tightened. The criticisms never seemed to stop. Well intentioned, sure, but she was sick of it. "I'm doing the best I can," she said as she opened the stroller. "Let's go."

A Lincoln Town Car pulled up behind them. Another car parked in the driveway, followed by a third. Down the street, a tall man and a young girl approached with a large bag of treats from a famous doughnut house.

"We're having a meeting," boomed Bart Quinn, coming to greet Alison and her parents. "It's a fundraiser for retired greyhounds." He turned toward the doughnut man. "This is Adam Fielding, our veterinarian, and he's

26

been working with the dogs but needs bigger facilities. Maybe you'll want to adopt one."

"Dogs?" asked Alison. "I have enough to do with a baby!"

The vet grinned. "Just you wait a bit. Kids and pets go together like peanut butter and jelly."

But Alison couldn't conceive of more responsibility, more work, more anything. She smiled and extended her hand. "Nice to meet you. I'm Alison Berg-Martin, over on Neptune Street."

He shook it. "Neptune? Then you must be near a friend of mine. Mike Romano? And of course, Sophie."

Oh, boy. "Across the street."

"Good. He's registered for our 5K run next week. Maybe you can join him." He handed her a flier. "Raise some money for us."

She took the flier and made polite chat. His little girl and Carol were walking Joey down the block and back. "Your daughter's really good with him. How old is she?"

"Sara's ten. She's wonderful with anything smaller than she is. Human or animal. My right-hand assistant."

"But not old enough to babysit?"

"Afraid not. Oh, there's Rebecca." His eyes lit up as he walked toward the brunette who emerged from Sea View House.

Alison recognized that light. That special light. The same as Peter's eyes every single time she'd entered a room. She blinked. "He loves her," she whispered. *Good luck to you both.*

"She's fighting it," said Bart. "But no matter. The magic is here. Adam is the right one for her. The poor lass, in the bombing and all."

She changed focus. "The marathon?"

"Aye. Lost a leg, but look at her now. She wants to run in our race next week, but Adam's not having it."

She could imagine the fireworks over that decision. Well, not her business.

"Good luck with the fundraising," she said, placing Joey in the stroller. "Time to hit the beach."

"Don't forget to join us next Sunday. Come with Mike," called Adam. "The whole town will be here. And we'll have fun."

"I can't promise, but I'll make a donation either way." She walked toward the corner and crossed the narrow street, which ran alongside the high dunes. On the far side of those dunes, the beach waited. She lifted Joey from the carriage while her mom pushed it, and her dad carried the umbrella and beach chairs.

"You need to make some friends," David said. "Run, jog, walk—whatever you want—but you should enter the 5K. You need to meet some young people."

Young people? She'd never be young again.

"Dad's right," said Carol. "Aren't Pete's folks coming to visit next weekend? You'll have built-in babysitters. And if they can't make it, we'll come back."

Why did everyone think they knew what was best for her? Mike, nagging her about the cello and her garden; her folks, nagging about friends. Only Joey was on her side. She cuddled him close.

"All you want is a mommy," she whispered and kissed him, thrilled to be the chosen one. She glanced at the others. "We'll see about next week," she temporized. "Today's an adventure, too. Our first day in the sand, sea, and sun. Right, Joey?"

"Which is a shame," said Carol. "If you'd made some friends with other young mothers…"

Alison sighed and tuned out her own mother.

##

The first thing Alison noticed when they arrived home that afternoon was the new flowers. Marigolds, zinnias, and petunias forming a front border of the garden. Such a happy look! Yellow, orange, and deep pink, which reinforced the roses behind them. Once everyone was out of the car, Alison walked closer and shook her head.

"I thought he was finished, but…wow."

"Wow is right," said her mom. "And those are annuals. They'll only last the season. He'll have to dig them up in the fall."

"And that's more work…I really have to pay him," said Alison, snatching Joey as he reached for the plants. "No picking, Joey. Mike's flowers."

Her son squirmed, turning his head back and forth. "Man. Man." Then started to cry.

"Why don't you invite Mike to dinner?" asked Carol. "If he won't take money, then offer him a good meal."

"I'd rather pay."

She ignored her mom's eye roll and urged everyone inside. Showers, baths, supper preparation. And later a ringing phone.

She inhaled a clean Joey and handed him to her dad. Quickly checking the readout, she sighed at seeing the garden center. She spoke before he had a chance.

"The flowers are beautiful. The whole garden is. I want you to send me a bill. An honest bill."

"Are your folks staying overnight?"

"Did you hear me?"

"Just answer the question, Red. Do you have a sitter?"

She eyed her parents, who were watching, listening, and waiting. Obviously identifying the caller without voluntary help from her. "I suppose I do, but I'm not going anywhere, thanks."

"Just once. Come out with me once, and I promise not to bother you again. I want you to hear some live music with good players, totally different from what you're used to."

She didn't play cello anymore and barely listened to the radio. And now, a live performance...? She would have loved it once, but...how could she treat herself to such pleasure now?

"I can't do it, Mike. I'm sorry."

"Consider it payment for the garden. And I hate the word *can't*."

"That's sneaky. Mean. And below the belt. You know the yard is gorgeous. That's so unfair of you. I'd rather write you a check." When her balance grew again next month.

"Nope. Doesn't work that way. I'll pick you up at seven."

##

He would have done the same for anyone. That's what Mike told himself as he showered and shaved that evening. It was a plus that Alison was easy on the eyes. But more important, he'd walked in similar shoes. He knew grief. He knew disappointment.

A boy needed a mom. He'd lost his when he was eleven, a kid who hadn't understood what was happening.

"We're a couple of bachelors now," his dad had said a year later, when the shock had begun to subside. "We've got a bachelor pad." But tears had run down Paul's face. They both knew the joke was weak. His dad had tried to make life as normal as possible for the young Mike. Friends were welcome, baseball, music, homework checks...every aspect of his day-to-day life remained intact. And it had helped. Especially baseball.

When he'd eyed the batter and wound up for a pitch, he'd thought of nothing else, not even his loving mom.

Alison, on the other hand, didn't have a handle on normal. Her son wouldn't know the difference at this point, but he would later. Protecting a toddler was necessary, but smothering a kid led to problems. The greatest gift she could give Joey was an ordinary life.

He rapped at Alison's front door. Her dad opened it and immediately stepped outside. "It's cooler on the porch, and besides, she's not ready. They're putting Joey down for the night." He gestured to a couple of chairs.

Mike sat and waited. The older man must have had something on his mind.

"I don't pretend to know why you're pursuing her," said David. "The real Alison—the exuberant, smiling Alison—has disappeared, and frankly, I doubt she's coming back."

"I never knew your *real* Alison," said Mike. "But what I do know is that this lady can use a friend."

The other man smiled. "Exactly right. Especially in a new place. Which I can't pretend to understand, either…but…" He sighed. "I love my daughter, so for God's sake, whatever you talk about, don't make things worse."

The door opened and Alison walked outside. Mike stood but couldn't speak. Wow. In a bright, sleeveless sundress, snug at the waist, long earrings, and strappy, low-heel sandals, Ali looked beautiful. No Cleopatra makeup. Just some lipstick. She didn't need to imitate a magazine model. He took it all in with one glance, wanted to shout praises, but stopped himself. *Play it cool or she'll run.*

"Not bad, Red. You clean up pretty well."

She blushed but waved him away. "You can thank my mom. She picked out the dress. I would have worn jeans."

David stepped forward and cupped his daughter's face. "You look wonderful. Just like always. Have a good time, will ya?"

"Do you have my cell number in your phone?"

He checked. "Yes, I do."

"Mom knows where everything is, but don't hesitate to call..." She made an impatient gesture with her hand. "I'll probably be back in an hour or so anyway."

"Is that right?" asked Mike.

She eyed him. "We'll see how it goes. The town's small. I can always walk if you're not ready to leave the place."

His muscles tensed, but he managed a chuckle. "You're not making it easy, are you?"

She stepped toward him. "This was your ridiculous idea, but it's not too late to back out."

Which was exactly what she wanted him to do. "Not a chance, Red." He reached for her hand, interlaced their fingers, and held his breath.

He felt her resist, but she didn't pull away.

CHAPTER FOUR

The club at the Wayside Inn was known as a musical hot spot every weekend during the season. Tonight was no different.

"The parking lot's almost full," Mike grumbled. "I should have called ahead for a table."

Alison shrugged. She would have been content to stay home. In the end, they were lucky. The hostess led them to a corner table within five minutes.

"Full dining room service in here, too," she said, leaving the menus. She glanced at her watch. "The group starts at eight."

"Perfect," said Mike. "We've got time to order." He passed a menu to Alison. "Whatever you want."

"I'm not very hungry," she said, glancing at the offerings. "Maybe a salad."

Mike sat back in his chair, his arms crossed. "Are you kidding? With all the other delicious options here? What's with you women, anyway? You all eat grass."

"Is that the voice of experience?" So she'd been right. He knew women.

"Experience, my eye! Just look around."

She did. Salads of all stripes decorated the tables. Greek, Cobb, Asian, Caesar. Some topped with chicken or shrimp. Salads here, salads there, salads grew up everywhere—Dr. Seuss played in her head. A giggle emerged. Then another. Then she couldn't stop.

She confessed to Mike, made up more "salad" verses, and this time shared laughter filled the space between them. Admiration shone in his blue eyes.

"I knew you could do it," Mike said. "Knew a sense of humor lurked inside you. And the music's still there, too."

She wanted to cry. She hadn't thought of Peter for an hour. He hadn't been sitting on her shoulder, keeping her company, as he always did. Mike had distracted her too well and…they'd laughed.

"You're allowed, you know," Mike whispered, stroking the top of her hand. "A little fun is allowed."

Maybe. Maybe once in a while. Later on.

She slipped her hand from under his and placed it in her lap. "We're not going there." No emotional confessions, no intimacy of any kind. Sharing was not allowed.

Despite her protest, however, she heard the questioning note in her voice, the uncertainty. Mike's brow rose. He must have heard it, too.

"Maybe not just yet," he said. "But I have confidence in you."

Suddenly, it wasn't a game, and she had to be fair to this man. "You're a nice guy, Mike…actually more than nice. You've got it all. But"—she shook her head—"I'm the wrong one."

##

She saw his rueful grin before a smile replaced it. "Have some steak, Red. And stop analyzing everything.

34

Typical classical musician. Everything by the book. Everything technically correct."

She sat straighter.

"Wait till you hear those guys," said Mike, nodding at the stage, where a piano and drum kit were standing. "With the bass and sax, you'll have the sweet sound of a jazz combo."

"Bass? Are you…?"

"No," he replied, shaking his head. "I was a pro ball player, not a pro musician. But I picked up the bass again since I've been home and usually jam with a few friends. We mix it up and have a good time. And"—he leaned toward her—"we've improved since high school!"

She couldn't picture herself "mixing it up." Improvising throughout an entire piece. Not with her training. "Sounds like fun."

He burst out laughing. "Stop being polite. You look like you just ate a lemon."

She didn't—couldn't—deny it, and was about to speak when a familiar couple headed their way. The woman from Sea View House. And the vet. "Your friends are here."

Mike stood and motioned them closer. "Want to join us?"

"That's what we'd hoped," said Adam Fielding. "We ate in the dining room and wanted to stay for some music. We misjudged the crowd."

"Sit down," invited Alison. "Rebecca, isn't it?"

"That's right. Nice to see you again." The woman carefully took her seat. "Stools are easier, but I'm learning."

"I'm so sorry about—about the bombing."

Rebecca shrugged. "Me, too. I was just in the wrong place, at the wrong time, and now I'm called a hero. No one realizes that all I want to do is hide!"

"Me, too," said Alison. "I definitely know that feeling."

"I can vouch for that," added Mike. "Getting Alison to come here was an accomplishment. I'm the hero tonight!"

Rebecca's glance flickered from one to the other. She grabbed Alison's hand. "You know, of course...you do understand...that we can't really hide or-or they win."

Alison's gaze locked on Rebecca's. She barely breathed.

"The bad guys," continued the woman. "The terrorists and drug dealers. They come in all shapes and sizes and ages. But we have to fight back."

Alison's spine straightened, her attention snagged. Rebecca had been down a horrific road, too. But now the woman blushed.

"Sorry to get carried away. It's not my business...everyone's different..."

"Know what Rebecca did two weeks ago?" chimed in Adam, his arm resting around Rebecca's shoulders, pride on his face. "She swam in Pilgrim Bay."

"What?" gasped Alison.

"I was scared to death," said Rebecca, "but being in the water was wonderful. Adam was wonderful." Her eyes shone. She seemed as ecstatic about the man as she was of her accomplishment. By his adoring expression, Adam seemed to feel the same way.

"She was very safe," said Adam. "We went out with Rachel and Jack Levine in their boat, and they both swim like fish."

But it sounded terrifying to Alison. Simply terrifying. Except for Peter, Rebecca was the bravest person Alison had ever known.

"How did you do it?" she whispered. "How did you cross over the line from frightened to brave?"

Rebecca shrugged. "I-I'm not sure. I tried to do it alone—the therapy, the chores. My whole life, I never asked for help. But…this time…somehow…it didn't work that way." She stared at Alison. "It just doesn't work that way."

Mike started to whistle a familiar Beatles tune, and Rebecca perked up. "Exactly right! It took a little help from my friends." Her gaze rested on Adam, her eyes looking suspiciously moist.

Rebecca's struggle had ended as a love story. But Alison had already had her love story. No amount of physical therapy or any therapy could change her ending. Having hundreds of friends would make no difference. Nothing could bring back her brave, loving, and devoted Peter. And nothing could lessen the shadow of her selfishness and guilt.

She'd wanted him to change units in the department. Did he have to work Narcotics? Couldn't he find something safer? Maybe Internet crime? Behind a desk? They'd argued about it on and off for months, including the day before he was killed.

The guys and I are a team, baby. We belong together, just like you and the orchestra.

So she hadn't told him about the baby they'd made together. About Joey. She'd been angry and wanted time to calm down, time to marshal new arguments for after she told him…so they could celebrate together. Selfish, selfish!

"That's the way it works in Pilgrim Cove," said Mike, drawing her back to the present. "To put it bluntly, everybody knows your business and butts in."

Alison heard herself chuckle, felt herself relax. "Perhaps that's not so bad after all."

"You're a slow learner, Red. That's what I've been trying to tell you all along."

Maybe she'd been wrong. Maybe Mike had been offering only a hand in friendship. But when she glanced up, his smile didn't reach his eyes.

##

He'd keep his distance for a while. Maybe forever. He and Alison would become friends and only friends because that's what she wanted.

The plan stank.

On the following Sunday, they ran in the Race for the Rescues, and Mike introduced Alison to a bunch of his friends. Rachel and Jack Levine, who'd taken Rebecca on their boat. Laura and Matt Parker, who owned the hardware store with his dad. Ali already knew Lila Parker but met her famous piano-man husband, Jason, younger brother of Matt. A family of musicians, actually. Everyone played a keyboard.

After the race, he and Alison returned to Neptune Street sweaty and exhausted.

"I had a good time, Mike. And I liked your friends. Thanks."

"You had more stamina than I thought. You surprised me."

"Well, I'm not a hothouse flower," she protested. "Taking care of Joey requires strength."

She looked so pretty with her shy smile, her face flushed. So adorable Mike actually forced his hand to remain at his side when he really wanted to stroke her cheek. She waved and stepped toward her own home. Her in-laws waited for her inside, and he shuddered at the problems his presence could create.

He entered his own house, whistled to Sophie, and called out to his dad, reading on the back porch. His decision to stay away from Red would begin right then.

His friends were all paired off. Couples. Married or soon to be if he guessed right about Rebecca and Adam. He suddenly felt old. Footloose. With no purpose. Which was ridiculous. His responsibilities were endless. He had a business to help run, fire to fight, and a bass to play. Too much damn thinking was dangerous. His life was full. Full enough, anyway. He hadn't known he'd been missing anything until Alison had moved in across the street and shaken him up.

He showered, dressed, and revved up his Harley.

"Where you going?" asked Paul, coming to the front steps. "I thought we'd grill some steaks."

"I've got some unfinished business at the batting cages." Maybe he'd hit one to China. "I'll be back in an hour."

"Damn it, son! You'll damage that shoulder again. But I see that stubborn look, so give me a helmet. You're not going alone."

His old man was the best. But… "I'll be fine, Dad. I'm not a child anymore."

"Are you kidding me? No matter how old you get, you'll always be *my* child." Paul grabbed the spare helmet and hoisted himself behind Mike. "And furthermore," he said, "I see you looking at the sweetheart across the street. In my opinion, your taste has improved a thousand percent. So, what are you going to do about her?"

His dad was right on. Until Alison, he'd spent his time playing games. Marking time with women who meant nothing while trying to become the Red Sox's starting pitcher.

He turned in his seat. "Alison's different. And I didn't even know there was a difference." He waved his arm in a broad gesture and said, "You know what I mean?"

He felt his shoulder being squeezed. "Ahh, Mike. I'm so sorry you missed out. Teenage boys need mothers to watch and learn from. They need moms as well as dads. How else can they tell an ordinary girl from the special one? After I met your mom—and I was older than most guys—there was no one else."

Mike stared at the house across the street. "I can't do anything about her, Dad, except offer a friendship. That's all she wants."

"She's still hurting, but she won't remain alone. She's young, a lot younger than I was when your mom died. Just give her time."

He'd do that. He had no appetite for club life anymore. No appetite for running around. So he had nothing to lose.

"Hang on, Dad." He revved the engine again and took off. Maybe he'd forget about her for an hour.

##

Alison watched Joey climb into the stroller and plop down, a look of pride on his face as if to say, *I did it!* So cute. She chuckled, strapped him in, and set out for the library as she'd been doing every Thursday morning during the summer. She glanced across the street, realizing that except for an occasional morning coffee and a high five with Joey, she hadn't seen much of her neighbor during the last few weeks. Well, summer was the busy season, and perhaps August signaled the garden center's getting-ready-for-autumn mode.

She walked down Neptune to Oyster Road and turned the corner. Now she had a straight shot to the library several blocks ahead. She glanced at her watch. Plenty of time to make the ten o'clock start.

But with all the *good mornings*, and chatting a bit with neighbors, they were almost late for story time. As she and Joey quickly took their places on the floor, smiling and waving to the other young moms in the room, satisfaction filled her. A sigh of relief. She nuzzled her son. "I think we're doing all right, baby boy. I think we're doing all right."

The hour sped by with stories and songs. After gathering up Joey and his new books, she looked for Lou Goodman, one of Bart Quinn's retired pals and Rachel Levine's dad. Lou had been the town's high school librarian, and now he volunteered at the public library every week. They usually visited before she left for home.

She spotted him walking swiftly toward her. "I was hoping you'd be here today," Lou said, leaning toward Joey and shaking the boy's hand. Joey's wide grin now sported two small rows of teeth.

"You're invited to lunch at the diner with some of my friends," said Lou. "The usual crowd. Bart, Max Rosen, and whoever else might be there."

Lovely men, but why? "Thanks...but..."

"Please don't say no. You're a sight for our sore eyes. Besides, we wanted to talk to you about something, and talking is always better over a meal."

Food hadn't been important to her for a long time, but she didn't argue the point. She leaned into the carriage.

"Want to eat in a real restaurant, Joey?" She had no clue about the "something" Lou mentioned, but if she couldn't oblige, she'd decline whatever it was...gracefully, of course.

The Diner on the Dunes was a landmark of the town, a one-story white clapboard building with a nautical feel thanks to the row of porthole-style windows near the roofline. Above the doorway hung a red-and-white wooden sign proclaiming *Home of the ROMEOs*. Alison chuckled to herself each time she saw it.

41

"There's your name, Mr. Goodman," she said, pointing at the nameplate. "I always think of the ROMEOs as Bart Quinn and his Gang of Elves."

Lou laughed; his eyes twinkled. "We think of ourselves that way, too. No one can best the Quinn."

They left Joey's stroller outside and made their way to the round table in the back of the eatery.

A *reserved* card sat in the center, but Joey claimed the center of attention after he climbed into his high chair, looked at his new companions, and declared, "Pa-pa, Pa-pa." He banged his little fists on the table and grinned at his fellow diners. Hands up to high five, and one by one, each man's expression softened as the "Papas" fell a bit in love with their new little friend.

"I guess he thinks every man with gray hair is Papa," Alison said, sitting down next to her son, "just like my dad and father-in-law."

"You should come around more often," declared Bart Quinn. "We're always ready for another little one in our midst."

Before Alison could reply, Joey chimed in again. "Man! Mike! Sophie." He looked around the table again before staring at his mom, his expression so perplexed it would have been comical had Alison seen the humor.

"Mike's working," she said.

"Work-ing," he repeated. "Flowers in dirt. Pretty."

Impressed, she stared at him and the men. "He's learning new words all the time."

"The boy's growing up," said Bart. "His vocabulary's growing as fast as he is. It won't take but a minute, and he'll be starting school."

A big knot filled her stomach. She eyed the old leprechaun. "Do you think you're telling me something I don't already know? But I'd rather not think about it." When Joey started kindergarten, life would change again. She preferred living one day at a time.

The old man leaned back in his chair, a contented smile spreading across his face. "You're the smartest one in the room, lass. Of course you know that time marches on. The healing started in Sea View House last year, and now you're making a life in Pilgrim Cove. That's progress."

The waitress appeared then and took their orders. Alison noted Bart leaving further conversation to others. The man knew how to push and retreat, push and retreat, just enough to shake a person up before backing off. She could see through him. She suspected his friends could, too. Sharp as knives, the lot of them.

After the waitress left, Doc Rosen took out a large manila envelope and put it down in front of him. The others became suspiciously quiet, and on the back of her neck, Alison felt her hair rise. On her skin, goose bumps.

"Lou and I have a problem," said Max Rosen. "And we're hoping you can help. In fact, we need you." He tapped the envelope.

"We're not sure you know, or are even aware, that the Jewish High Holy Days are next month."

She cocked her head. "I do know—not the exact dates—but they're always in the fall." Smiling, she added, "I come from a mixed heritage on my dad's side. And my Jewish grandfather"—she swallowed hard—"was the one who…" And suddenly she couldn't speak. Couldn't explain how her Papa's violin connected them. How he'd played for her and taught her, and cheered when she eventually chose the cello. He'd approved of Emanuel Shilling, her teacher, who'd gifted her with the instrument that now lay dormant in her home. Playing duets with her Papa…such happy days! Gone now. Just like her days with Peter.

Looking around the table, she said, "I adored my grandfather, and he adored me. But I also have a lot of friends from all backgrounds. So I know about holidays."

A grin spread across Lou's face. "Right, right," he said, turning to Doc Rosen. "Show her what we have, and let her tell us yes or no." Lou smiled at her. "It's for Yom Kippur, the Day of Atonement, the holiest day of our year."

Doc opened the envelope and drew out a sheaf of paper with musical notation. He thrust the package at Alison. "Can you read this?"

She glanced at the top margin of the sheet. *For cello.* Of course she could read it. Her sight-reading was excellent. She examined it again and felt a tiny smile coming through. She not only knew this music, she'd played it years ago. The piece was the famous "Kol Nidre", arranged by Bruch, the music that traditionally set the tone and began all the prayers on that holiest of days.

She flipped to the next page and found another work. "Avinu Malkeinu." Both pieces were haunting, ethereal, and meaningful to the human heart. A decade earlier, as a college student, she'd accepted a request from a local synagogue, so eager she was to make music for an appreciative audience…and earn a little extra, too. Additional music lay behind these two pieces.

Her own small congregation in the diner seemed to be holding their collective breath as they waited for her response. She raised her head and stared at Doc Rosen. At Lou Goodman. Both kind and sweet men, still taking care of their town. And needing help doing it.

"I can read this, and I can teach it to someone." There. She'd offered a little something to them. She wanted to cooperate. *But please, gentlemen, please don't ask me to play.*

"But we have no one else!" said Doc Rosen. "The cellist we hired months ago just broke his contract with us. The ritual committee has contacted every school of music in the area—and there are many—but we're too late because the holidays are only a month away."

Lou Goodman, her library friend, leaned toward her. "We can't even imagine Yom Kippur without the cello. The cantor blends the traditional melodies that have been around for a thousand years with the more contemporary. All generations are satisfied. The singing is wonderful, but with the cello, the music elevates the soul."

His appeal was eloquent, but she couldn't speak.

"They need you, lassie," said Bart.

Dots of perspiration covered her. Her hands felt clammy. Her bow would slip right through her fingers. "I-I'm not…"

"Do it, Red," ordered a male voice behind her, "and come out of the shadows."

She twirled in her seat. Father and son Romano stood behind her. She was ready to blast Mike, regardless of his dad being on hand, until she saw his eyes. So dark and shadowed the normally bright blue seemed black. Maybe a little tired. He held up his hand in a stop motion and leaned in.

"I'm not your boss, but I am your friend, and I know what I see. What I sense. And what I sense is fear. So pick up the damned music and make a bunch of people happy. Isn't that what your gift is all about?"

She'd been on the verge of taking the sheaf home. This music was for a purpose bigger than herself and her personal troubles. Mike's "bunch of people," including the three lovely men at the table, looked forward to a sacred time and place, to their spirits being lifted from daily routines, lifted beyond themselves for a special time out of time. Prayer, forgiveness, peace. True, she couldn't find it for herself, never would, but if she could

45

be a conduit for others…? Maybe that would be her salvation.

Mike was now holding Joey, who had gone into paroxysms of happiness after spotting his "man." Alison ignored them both and spoke directly to Lou and Doc Rosen.

"I'll try. I'll try to do well. But I cannot promise the results." She gathered the music to her and carefully replaced it in the manila envelope. Then she raised her chin and glared at Mike. "My decision has nothing, absolutely nothing, to do with you…*friend*."

To her surprise, a wide smile crossed Mike's face. "Even better," he said.

CHAPTER FIVE

Mike placed Joey back into the high chair before he and his dad sat down at the ROMEO table. He heard Alison sigh. If it weren't for Joey being hungry, he figured she would have asked for a to-go box. But the baby was digging into his mac 'n cheese with gusto, pausing only to drink some milk from his sippy cup. Sippy cup? The baby wasn't the only one learning new words.

His yawn took him by surprise. "Wow. I need that coffee."

"Out too late?" snapped Alison.

He glanced sharply at her but decided to ignore the attitude. "An all-nighter at the firehouse. Every Wednesday."

"Oh, sorry," she said, sounding contrite. "Maybe you should order two cups of coffee."

Of course she thought he'd been partying. Perhaps she'd picked up on his restlessness lately. Nah. They hadn't seen each other much. He leaned into the toddler. "Hey, Joey?"

"Mike, Mike, Mike." The boy's wide grin would melt any heart. Mike bent down and kissed him. "Mommy thinks I'm a really bad boy. But you don't, do you?"

Joey responded with a long mix of English and baby English that made everyone laugh. Mike looked at Alison. "See? He knows the truth." He looked at the child. "Thanks, Joey. High five." They suited action to words. Alison chuckled and Mike relaxed.

Bart Quinn reached for Alison's hand. "Ah, lassie. I told you a long time ago that Mike was one of the good guys."

"I remember, but the only good guy in my life right now is this little boy." Her sweet smile at Bart plucked a small jealous chord in Mike—and the man could be her grandfather! She covered Joey with kisses down his neck and across his cheek. "Love you so much," she whispered.

Oh, yeah.

"And speaking of sons," said Paul Romano slowly, "I've got a surprise for mine."

Mike focused like a laser on his dad. What surprise? The business was running like a top. The house was paid off. Health? No. He wouldn't make a public announcement about a health issue. A woman after all this time? Nah, not likely. Mike would have known. After all, he and his dad shared a house.

Paul sat back in his chair and smiled at his friends. "You guys are having all the fun in this town. I've been doing some thinking lately and decided it's time for me to join the ROMEOs."

Mike looked from his dad to Bart and back to his dad. "The ROMEOs? But that means…"

"I'm going to officially retire. So at the end of the year, the business will be all yours. Nice and legal."

A deep silence was followed by cheers, well wishes, and the promise of a new business card for the ROMEOs.

Mike said nothing. Couldn't find words.

"Cat got your tongue?" asked Alison.

"A little warning would have been nice."

Her eyebrows rose; her mouth tightened. She stared at him and said, "But shocks *aren't* nice. You just have to suck them up." She placed her hand over his, and he felt the burn. "This is not life-and-death," she said softly. "Romano's Landscape and Design seems like a healthy business."

But not his first choice. He didn't reply, still digesting his dad's decision. Trying to understand it, and succeeding too well. Paul's retirement was all Mike's fault. His shoulder had hurt after batting practice, and his dad had witnessed his pain. In response, Paul had killed any lingering dreams Mike nurtured of returning to the game he loved. If Mike had chosen a path in broadcasting or coaching, his dad wouldn't have stood in his way, but neither career had tempted him.

After a year of therapy and a year working out at home, hoping against hope, he was staring at a clean break with the past. His dad was a smart guy with clearer vision than Mike. He turned his hand so that Alison's was tucked into his. At the same time, he felt the weight of Paul's arm around his shoulder.

"You never know how the conversation will unfold at the diner," said Mike. "You shocked the heck out of me, Dad."

Paul cleared his throat. "Since you've been home, you've helped me grow the business quite a lot. In fact, it's phenomenal, son. I-I hope that even if you're not cheering now, you'll be happy." He emitted a deep sigh. "That's all I want. For you to be healthy and happy."

"Hear, hear." Bart raised his mug of coffee. "To new beginnings. To health and happiness for all our children."

Mike leaned into Alison, glad her hand still rested in his. "They're looking at you, too, Red."

##

Alison had thought Pilgrim Cove would offer an escape from the real world. It offered the ocean, sky, gulls. The beaches and sea breezes. The friendliness and security of a cozy cocoon.

But she'd been wrong. Her problems sat perched on her shoulder, shadows that traveled with her.

The manila envelope lay on the kitchen table for the rest of the day, a constant reminder of what she'd have to do next. A constant cause of clammy palms and a prickle of tension. Laughable. She'd seen the music. Sure, it was challenging, but not more than other pieces she'd learned and perfected, the solos she'd performed with the South Shore Philharmonic from Beethoven's symphonies, Prokofiev's *Romeo and Juliet Suite*, and Rosini's "William Tell." Plus so many others. The file cabinet in her mind began to open to musical memories, auditions, practice sessions…and her dear, wonderful teacher, Emanuel Shilling.

Evening deepened and temperatures dropped a few degrees. Always a pleasure that surprised her at the coast. Joey went down for the night, and Alison saw no reason to postpone her visit to the living room, rarely used, where her cello lay on its back, secured in its hard case. With a chair and music stand nearby, she took a deep breath, unlocked the case, and lifted the instrument. She loosened the end pin screw, releasing the rubber-tipped spike that anchored the cello to the floor while in use.

First, she'd clean it…for the second time this week. Working slowly, she admitted that procrastination was an art, too. One soft cotton cloth for the instrument's body, another one for the strings. Gently, gently, she wiped the cello's front and back from neck to end pin. She'd clean it to perfection.

"You're such a beauty," she whispered. "The congregation will love you." And they would if she could calm her nerves and do justice to both the music and the instrument. Maybe Peter would hear her. Maybe he'd been listening for her all this time. And maybe pigs really could fly.

She sighed, now impatient with herself, impatient with living in the past. He was gone and she couldn't fix that. But maybe she could fix Doc Rosen and Lou Goodman's problem. She tightened the bow and applied rosin. Then sat behind the instrument and tightened the strings. The sheet music lay spread across the stand before her. Everything felt so familiar—her position behind the cello, the bow in her hand, and the anticipation.

With the first downstroke, her senses awakened. And she was only running through a C major scale. But in moments, she turned to the music and was lost in her old world, another world, totally enveloped by the piece. She played on, interpreting and trying again, giving expression to the almost-forgotten melodies. She pictured her grandfather from years ago, heard the vibrato in his voice as he prayed and sang, her little-girl self at his side, happy to be with him.

Soon, however, her bow was choosing other melodies—excerpts from Beethoven's Fifth, part of a Brahms sonata, the young Juliet excerpt from Prokofiev. Despite the open window, her palms were damp. After three hours, her body was drenched and tears ran down her face. She sat quietly, holding the bow in one hand, the cello in the other. Pleasure marked with pain. And guilt.

Peter. Peter. Maybe she hadn't been cut out to be a cop's wife. Except…she'd loved him so much. She wished they hadn't argued that night. She wished she'd told him about Joey. That last was the worst. He'd had a right to know.

What was the point of wishing? She had to focus on the possible.

She'd play for Lou and Doc Rosen and the congregation—she couldn't refuse these lovely men— then take a final bow.

Through the open window, she heard the sound of clapping. "Bravo, Red," came a low voice. "I knew you had it in you."

"You know nothing," she whispered, wanting to fly at him. But the cello came first and had to be handled carefully. By the time she opened her front door, Mike was across the street.

She turned on her porch light and waited. He pivoted and made a beeline for her.

Alison watched him approach, his eager step bringing him quickly to her side. Moonlight illuminated the area while lamplight illuminated Mike and his five-o'clock shadow. Broad shoulders filled out his jersey, and his legs filled out his jeans just right.

"You're the real thing," he began with no small talk first, "and it's time to come out of hiding." He stepped closer and squeezed her hands. Sincerity shone on his face, his smile wide. "The music you make"—he shook his head—"unbelievable. You need to be back in the game. Back in Boston."

Her business was not his business. She wanted to pull away, but his honesty stopped her. No hidden agenda here. He spoke as a friend. And maybe she needed a true friend. Or maybe she wanted one.

She tilted her head back and smiled. "Thank you. But I like Pilgrim Cove. And"—she took a shaky breath—"and I think I-I might like Neptune Street." Her words ended on a whisper when she saw the proud light in his eyes. Pride in her.

"I do...too." She didn't move as his hands traveled slowly to her shoulders, his fingers leaving goose bumps in their wake.

She shivered, and he drew her close. . .closer. His head came down, blocking out the moon, the lights, and all else around them. She held her breath, waiting....

Waiting? Had she been waiting for this? Her hands cupped his waist; her eyes closed the moment before his lips found hers. Smooth, exploring, tasting...asking.

Rising on her tiptoes, she answered.

She didn't think about it, just let herself go. His thigh touched her hip and her pulse raced. He was taller, bigger, but as lean and tight as her husband. The man wasn't Peter, not on the outside. But on the inside lived a person with a heart and a soul who knew how to laugh. Who teased her and made her laugh. Who respected her work. And for all those qualities, the ones she'd noted and stored away in the basement of her mind, he reminded her of another man. He reminded her of Peter.

No wonder she'd responded to him. His gentle kiss became harder and more urgent, and she matched his eagerness. Then he stepped back. The mild August evening could not explain the shiver that passed through her. Nor the disappointment.

She heard his intake of breath and his exhale. His lips were rigid, his stare blank. He didn't seem like a man who'd wanted to end their kiss.

"What...?" she began.

"I don't mind, but do you want to be the talk of the neighborhood?" A brief smile appeared as he nodded at the empty street.

And just like that, reality seeped in. She was enthusiastically kissing a man who was not Peter, and a wave of guilt drenched her. She put up her hand and stepped back.

"I'm sorry...I-I can't..." She turned toward the door.

"But you will. One day. And soon. Because you're alive, Red. And that's a precious gift."

Maybe he wasn't the right man. Always a possibility. Mike let himself into the house, called to his father, and reached for the phone. Jason Parker wouldn't mind a late call, not when music was involved, not when a fundraising concert for the marathon victims was also involved.

Alison wouldn't stop playing after her gig at the temple if he could help it. She wouldn't lose her career the way he had his. Her passion for the cello matched his for a bat, ball, and glove, especially on the mound. Only a calamity could have stopped either of them, and it had. But Alison could reclaim her career, her future. While he...? He rotated his shoulder, felt the ache, and thrust out his chin. He had to own his reality. His dad had been one step ahead of him.

Running a successful business was not to be sneezed at, and he had his own ideas for expansion. He wasn't a newbie; he'd grown up in the business. Every minute not playing ball was spent with his dad in the garden center. Second best might work out just fine. Second best had him working hard all day and sleeping like a baby at night. Except for Wednesdays. His commitment to the firehouse and his fellow EMTs was sacrosanct.

"In my opinion, Jason, she's the real thing," he said into the phone. By the time he hung up, the piano man was on board, ready to listen and waiting for Mike's call to visit Neptune Street one evening. No fuss. No fanfare. Mike hoped he'd gauge correctly about Alison's new evening routine of practice sessions, and that she'd continue to keep her window open!

The next night, the instrument's mellow tones floated through the air, starting about nine o'clock. And two evenings later, Jason Parker joined Mike and a few neighbors sitting quietly on beach chairs along the sidewalk, enjoying the concert.

"She's acquired an audience," whispered Mike, "but if they applaud, I bet she'll stop."

The music started before Jason could respond. First, the pieces for the synagogue and then the classical repertoire solos.

"I want her for the fundraiser," said Jason. "She'll touch everyone's heart just as the honorees will. Maybe for the processional…the theme from *Chariots of Fire*…or maybe Mariah Carey's "Hero"…maybe a duet with Luis…not sure yet…"

Mike chuckled, recognizing headliner Luis Torres as the pop singer who Jason credited for making him famous. Jason's eyes closed, and Mike guessed the man's mind was in a creative space, fluid and open, waiting for the best ideas to come. And they would. The musician had recruited talent, and was producing, directing, and performing in the concert, not an easy task.

"She can use my studio for practice," Jason finally said.

Mike nodded at the reference to the recently built facility on Main Street. "She also has a baby."

Jason smiled. "So do I. We just schlep her along in her carrier."

"Her son's almost two years old, not three months like little Rosemary. Cute and smart but...he can be a handful." A funny handful. Joey had a way of making him laugh. Mike was sure the boy understood far more than he could articulate.

"You're smiling." The other man eyed him, looked toward the house, then back at Mike. A furtive gleam appeared. "So, how do you feel about...two-year-olds?"

##

A low hum of voices, people shuffling to find seats, an occasional cough. Alison glanced up from her place front and right of the congregation. A full house. She nodded in recognition. Always a full house during the high holy days. It was a new year, a new beginning, a new chance to be a better person in the following year.

A better person? Maybe for them. For these smiling but serious congregants who gathered as a community to start anew. She'd be lucky just to hang on and maintain her equilibrium.

She spotted Lou walking toward her, a woman following. The man looked dapper in his navy blue suit and white prayer shawl draped over his shoulders. Her grandfather had worn a similar tallit. She smiled at the librarian.

"Very handsome, Mr. Goodman."

His cheeks reddened. "This is my wife, Pearl."

The woman leaned over and kissed Alison's cheek. "Thank you so much for doing this. Please join us for a break-the-fast dinner tomorrow night at our home. We always host an open house for our friends, and children are definitely welcome."

"I'll-I'll let you know. My parents might still be here, too."

"Bring them." Waving at her, they went to find seats.

Alison gazed at her music, then at the rabbi, and finally, the cantor, who would lead the congregation in song as well as chant prayers alone. When she'd met with the woman earlier in the month, Alison realized that her cello would be needed throughout the service and that Lou Goodman had misrepresented her responsibilities. Maybe he didn't realize?

She didn't mind. She'd begun playing again, could do justice to the music. If her grief and guilt still haunted her…well, she'd learn to live with it.

With her eyes on the cantor, she heard a last-minute rustle before the doors to the sanctuary closed. The room became quieter. She picked up her bow…and began.

Within two bars, silence reigned in the congregation. She felt the familiar atmosphere of an audience settling in for a concert. Opening their minds and hearts. Flying with her to another world. Here, a world of yearning and remorse for past wrongs, but also, a glimpse of redemption.

She gave them the best she had in her, her own heart yearning for the same things they prayed for in the new year. Peace, compassion. Forgiveness. She jerked in her seat. Yes, that was it! Forgiveness.

Peter, Peter. I am so sorry. Can you ever forgive me?

Her hands shook, she missed a note, but felt a veil of warmth surround her, and her heart fluttered with hope. And the promise of peace.

She quickly found her place in the score and continued on. It's what she'd been trained to do.

It's what a person does after a life blow. It's what my loving and generous husband would want me to do. Continue on. Continue to live.

She would begin anew for the second time.

Two hours later, as the sanctuary slowly emptied of people, Alison began repacking her cello. Whatever fatigue she might have felt after such focused playing dissipated when she spotted her parents. Her parents? And Mike Romano. And Jason Parker. Not to mention Bart Quinn.

Who was watching Joey?

By the time she secured the instrument and snapped the case shut, she was surrounded by her personal visitors. She craned her neck, seeking…

"Where's—"

"My dad's with him," said Mike before she could complete her question. "Said he's raised one boy and could handle another. Did you think we'd leave Joey alone?"

She hadn't considered it at all!

"Darling, you were wonderful," said her mom.

"The old Alison is back." Her dad's smile formed on trembling lips. His hug almost smothered her.

"Maybe…maybe," she admitted, amazed she hadn't noticed any of them in the congregation "Maybe my other self is on her way."

She grasped her cello case, but before she took a step, Jason Parker intercepted her.

"Loved what I heard. You've got it all, and I want you for the One Fund concert. To raise money for the bombing victims. There's no pay—everyone's

58

volunteering—but I'll cover expenses…music and…uh…babysitting. We've got TD Garden reserved the week before Christmas at no charge."

Her mind spun. Three months. Rehearsal time. Working with other musicians. Being back in Boston. Challenging, scary, but also exciting. And Rebecca Hart would benefit as well as all the other injured. She could do it.

She glanced at the hopeful faces around her. Felt their uniform vibration urging her to say yes. She closed her eyes for a moment's privacy. This very first decision after such an emotional evening had to be her own. Her hands tightened around the case. The cello. Part of her identity. Her first grown-up love. Before Peter, before Joey.

Opening her eyes, she said, "I played tonight because…it was for new friends and-and a holy purpose."

"And the streets of Boston are not holy ground?" Mike argued as if preparing for a debate. As though sensing her closing down.

She ignored him and extended her hand to Jason. "Of course I'll play for you."

"That's my girl." Mike's eyes gleamed with pride and something else. Something she wouldn't think about that night. Nor the next one. No jumping into deep waters like the adventurous Rebecca, who was now Mrs. Adam Fielding. Alison needed to wade in slowly, step by step, and feel her way back to normalcy. Whatever that would be now.

Mike didn't seem to expect a reaction to his "that's my girl" remark. Instead he faced his friend and grinned. "She's gonna knock it right out of the park, Jase."

Oh, why did he have to remind her so much of Peter?

CHAPTER SIX

In the garden center on Tuesday morning, Sophie whined at Mike and trotted to the front of the store. Her tail wagged so hard she could have powered sailboats across the water. Mike tracked her and saw Alison and Joey enter, the toddler strapped in his stroller.

"Well, this is a great surprise," he said, joining them. "I don't remember you ever visiting before."

Her blush was adorable. "That's changing as of now. I'm taking over the yard. You've done so much for me; it's time to give you a break."

Dang! He didn't want a break. "I enjoy it. Not to worry."

"Nope. In fact, I bought myself a mower yesterday."

Sweat broke out on the nape of his neck. "What do you know about power mowers? You can lose a hand…" Her hands! Her music.

But she was shaking her head. "I bought a push mower. Nice and safe. It'll give me a workout."

He touched her upper arms, searching for muscle. "Oh, yeah," he chuckled. "Just remember, I'm your backup."

Her lips compressed; her eyes sparkled. "I can do it. You'll see." She looked around. "So, where's the free class you're giving? That's what I came for."

"You're taking a class?" What had gotten into her? He'd bet she barely knew one flower from another. Glancing at his watch, he said, "Five minutes before you learn all about how to prepare your gardens for winter." Waving at other customers, he was about to leave, then turned back.

"Hey, Red. This new hobby of yours…it's not at the expense of your music, is it?"

"No! Of course not…" She shook her head, avoided his eyes. "I didn't realize how much I missed it," she whispered, "until I played again. So…thank you for that, Mike."

He wanted to kiss her senseless. She was beautiful inside and out. Heat climbed to his face, and he turned. "You would have gotten there without my push. You're the real deal, Red."

She laughed, didn't protest the nickname, which made him wonder about her even more. Something had changed. She seemed different.

"I see others gathering down near the mulch," she said. "Is that where the class will be held?"

He nodded.

"Now don't be late, Professor." Grinning, she pushed the stroller down the aisle.

As he watched her walk away, a mental light bulb turned on, and he wanted to cheer. *This* was the Alison her dad had talked about. The real Alison. A more confident and happy Alison.

And *this* Alison was fair game. All he had to do was win her heart.

##

"Clean up and cover up."

Alison took notes, lots of notes, thankful Sophie decided to stay next to the stroller, keeping Joey amused.

Until now, she'd always identified Mike as a ball player, out on the mound in the sunshine, focused on winning a game. She'd been narrow-minded. The man had more facets than a diamond, a complex guy who'd graduated from the Stockbridge School of Agriculture at UMass. No wonder his dad had the confidence to turn the business over to his son.

Preparing bulbs...

Preparing trees...

Preparing perennials...

Her hand hurt from writing by the end of the lecture, and dismay filled her as she reviewed her "assignments." She heaved a long sigh.

"Looks like we'll be spending a lot of time outdoors, Joey. Who knew gardens could be so complicated?"

"It's easier than you think, Red. Just a lot of words to explain, but the doing isn't so bad." His eyes gleamed; a warm smile crossed his face, making her breath hitch.

"When you know nothing," she managed to reply, "it's all hard. But if next year's blossoms compare to this year's...then it'll be worth it. You did such a beautiful job."

"Mike! Mike! Mike!"

The man lifted Joey from the carriage. "Hey, Joe. Want to play in some dirt?"

Alison watched Joey bounce in Mike's arms. Content. Happy.

"How about a horsie ride?"

In an instant, Joey was on Mike's shoulders, glee all over his face. "Go, horsie, go."

She watched them take off down the aisle and shook her head. Her neighbor had turned out to be a good guy and basically good for her son. Sure, the two grandfathers provided male role models, but...was it enough for a young boy?

Sighing, she admitted it would have to be. She was the parent. The sole parent, and she couldn't count on anyone else. Not even Mike. She'd play the hand she'd been dealt to the best of her ability. Joey by day. Her cello at night.

A new plan, a good plan. Workable for her and secure for Joey...in fact, secure for them both. *Until something else happened.* Because something always did. Nothing was forever.

Looking up, she spotted Bart Quinn at the counter, a beautiful bouquet of cut flowers in his hands.

"Going courting?" she teased.

"No...no," he said slowly. "It's for an old friend of mine. She's in the hospital, just had a surgery."

Next time, she'd keep her mouth shut. "I'm sorry, Mr. Quinn."

"Ach, it's the way of it. Her little Bonnie is living at Sea View House with her teacher for now. Kindergarten is a very big deal." He chuckled. "And Joy MacKenzie is the best."

The name sounded familiar, but Alison was sure she'd never met the woman. "The tenants keep changing, don't they?"

"That's the purpose, lass. A safe haven for those who need it."

"And don't I know that," said Alison, slowly nodding. "When I look back...I think I was numb."

Bart leaned in. "The trick is not looking back too much." He finished paying for his flowers and put his wallet away. "The point is to go on like you did this week. Your music...well, Jason hasn't stopped talking about you."

"Thanks," she whispered. "I'm still sort of getting used to...being back."

"But you won't be back until you're sitting first chair in the cello section," said Mike, joining them with Joey still on his shoulders, fingers twined in his hair.

"Slow down, neighbor," said Alison, reaching for the toddler. "I was second chair, and now my music is a night pursuit. Part-time only."

Mike rolled his eyes. "You've got to be kidding me." He turned to the older man. "Did you hear that, Bart? Back me up here."

The king of the ROMEOs, kisser of the Blarney Stone, seemed to be tongue-tied. "Oh, no, boyo. You're doing fine on your own." He slapped Mike on the shoulder. "I think you're able to handle this one just like..." He paused. "Have you been to Sea View House lately?"

"Sure," said Mike.

"Well, my money's on Logan Nash. Joy doesn't have a chance." His eyes shone bright blue as he looked from Mike to Alison. "I think I'll lay some wagers on which one of you couples tie that knot first."

The old man marched out the door with a spring in his step and a smile on his face.

"He should be arrested!" Alison felt her face flame with heat, but Mike just laughed.

"Typical Bart. Loves to stir up trouble."

"Well, don't get any ideas," ordered Alison.

Mike stepped back, hands up, palms out. "Me?" He moved closer. "When it comes to you, Red, I don't need help from anyone. My ideas are all my own." And then he kissed her. Lightly. On the lips. In front of the entire store. "See what I mean?"

The rest of Alison's day was a blur. *That kiss*. That kiss stayed on her mind. Sweet but firm. Respectful… Really? In public! Daring and dangerous.

Over-thinking. That's what she was doing. Ridiculous to over-think a little kiss that meant nothing. Or did it? Maybe a guilt-free kiss meant something…significant. Round and round she went, finally convinced it had been a sweet, simple kiss between friends. Period.

But she'd liked it.

And that's what bothered her.

Nothing bothered her, however, when she made music. After putting Joey down for the night, she scurried to her cello, eager to begin her practice session. She now worked full bore each evening, motivated not by the need to prove anything but by the joy of playing exquisite music and creating beauty. Little by little she was returning to the skill level she'd mastered by the time she'd lost Peter. Her satisfaction knew no bounds. He'd be proud of her.

Three hours appeared to be her sweet spot. In the old days, it would have been six, broken into sessions during the day. When preparing for a concert, she'd worked as hard as necessary.

As she put the bow down for the evening, she heard the soft jingle of Sophie's collar on the porch. With a smile, she opened the door.

"Hi…"

Without a word, his mouth came down on hers. "I thought about you all day," he murmured between tastes.

She couldn't speak. Not when her legs quivered and her breath disappeared. Not when a flame ignited inside. So familiar and yet…so new and exciting. On tiptoes now, she reached for more, her hands on his broad shoulders, her mind blank, her body on fire. His lips crushed hers. Hungry for her. She knew it, felt it, and her arms tightened around his neck. He led her inside and closed the door.

His breath came in short pants. His blue eyes seemed black under the hallway light. "No more treating you like a china doll," he said, his voice raspy. "And a broken doll at that." Cupping her cheeks, he said, "To me, you're a real, live woman. A strong woman. That's what I see now. And whether we strike out or hit a home run, I'm willing to chance it. The question is…are you?"

Strike out? A chance for things to go wrong. Again. She didn't want to think about a future. No planning ahead. She just wanted to live in the *now*. With Mike. He was a good guy, a man with a big heart, who embraced those in his orbit. She trusted him.

But still, the shaky smile she offered him was the best she could do. "Don't jump ahead. I'm a one-day-at-a-time kind of girl," she said. "I-I can't think about"— she gestured broadly—"down the road. Taking risks."

He held her gaze for a long minute. "Sooner or later, bad stuff happens to everyone. And it sucks. Yet folks manage to get up every morning, until a month passes, then a year and then…" He gazed across the street. "My dad went on. Bart went on."

She squeezed his hand. "Alone. They went on alone."

"They had kids—if that counts."

She glanced up toward Joey's room. "Oh, it counts, but running their businesses probably saved their sanity. Maybe my cello will save mine. But in the meantime…kiss me again."

"Yes, ma'am," he said with laugh. "Today, tomorrow, and next week. I'll be happy to oblige."

##

A week later—a lovely week of casual dinners with Mike at her house or at the Romanos', followed by her usual practice session—Alison strapped Joey into his car seat and headed toward the pier. She and Karen had finally worked out a visit where her friend could stay overnight. The late October sun provided a lingering warmth to the season that would soon give way to winter. The cold, dark season in New England. This year, Alison vowed, it would be a play-in-the-snow season.

To her surprise, the dock was busy at noon with passengers waiting to board as soon as the ferry pulled in. The boats ran every thirty minutes. Commuting to and from Boston by ferry was not only cool but efficient.

"Ferry boat. That's a ferry boat," she said to Joey, holding him up to see as soon as they got out of the car.

"Boat…boat. Water. Birds. Down, Mommy. Down. Me walk. Me run."

"No, Joey." Images of Joey falling into the bay mocked her.

She continued to hold him in her arms, not as easy now as when they'd moved to Pilgrim Cove. He'd grown taller and put on weight just as he should have. No matter how tired her muscles, however, she'd hang on to him.

"Sing with me Joey. Row, row, row the boat…" she began.

"Row, row, row the boat…" Joey mimicked.

He had a good ear. His words became adorably garbled, but his pitch was true. They sang until Alison noticed some familiar faces.

"There's Mr. Quinn and his friends. Let's say hello." The ferry would take a few more minutes to dock, and she welcomed the distraction of a ROMEO encounter.

Bart, Doc and Marsha Rosen, Rick and Dee O'Brien, Lou and Pearl Goodman were all dressed up for Boston.

"We've got season concert tickets for Tuesday afternoons," explained Bart. "We've been going for years. Pops in the summer and symphony in the winter."

Smiles on every face. "Retirement seems like a treat," said Alison, remembering the occasional afternoon she'd filled in for an absent cellist. Demanding performances, but exciting and fun. Great audiences of appreciative senior citizens.

"Every performance is a treat," said Mrs. Rosen as she rubbed Joey's hand. "Hey, big boy. Listen to this: Bom-bom-bom…bom." She sang the iconic first four notes of Beethoven's Fifth Symphony.

"Bom-bom-bom…bom!" repeated the toddler, earning cheers from everyone.

His wide grin made Alison laugh, and he repeated the four notes. "Good job, Joey. Very good." Maybe she should buy a keyboard for him.

The crowd meandered toward the ferry, and Alison spotted Karen, tote bag on her shoulder, violin case sticking out. Knowing her friend, she probably brought the Beethoven duet parts with her. The violin and cello made a wonderful pair.

"Seems like I'll be playing today, too." She waved at her neighbors. "Have a great time. Enjoy, enjoy." Then she ran toward her friend, took one look at Karen's familiar face, and a thousand ghosts rushed at her in a kaleidoscope of memories. Tears sprang unexpectedly.

"Looks like I arrived in the nick of time," said Karen, wiping her own eyes. She turned to Joey. "And look what I brought you, little man." She reached into her tote and pulled out a colorful wooden xylophone. "Want to make some music?"

"Glad it wasn't a drum," whispered Alison, giving Karen a quick hug.

"That, my friend, may come later."

##

A familiar rap on the front door preceded Mike's voice calling out a greeting. The rap and the voice. So familiar now. As though no distance existed between one front porch and the other. It was after dinner, and Alison quickly let him in. The gleam in his eye made up for the lack of a kiss.

"You could have joined us," she said after making introductions. "I didn't cook fancy for Karen."

"You don't cook fancy for me, either," said Mike with a grin. "And have I ever complained?"

"Wouldn't do you any good if you did," responded Alison, noting Karen's raised brow, her interest as she looked from one to the other as if at a tennis match.

Mike reached for Joey, who was all over Sophie. "Don't I get a hug? Or only the puppy?"

"Up. Up." The toddler reached high and Mike swung him around.

"Show Mike what Karen brought you today."

The boy wriggled to the floor and returned with his xylophone. "Look, Mike." He began to bang out and sing his row-the-boat song.

"Good job, kiddo. You're a good player."

"Sing, Mike. You sing wif me."

Mike laughed. "Need some male company, huh?" But he complied. "Let's try 'Take me out to the ball game'…"

"Ball, ball. Play ball wif me." And they disappeared to the enclosed front porch.

Silence reigned in the kitchen. Alison sensed Karen's curiosity and concern, and preempted her questions.

"I'm figuring it out. No promises, no commitments."

"That's wise. You and Pete...but it's been over two years now..."

"Two years and three months."

"Right. Long enough to throw caution away." She paced the room, then pivoted toward Alison. "Just as long as tall, dark, and handsome isn't the reason you're hiding away here."

Her spine straightened. "If I wanted Boston, I'd figure it out. But I want Pilgrim Cove. Mike's become a good friend, in fact, a great friend." *And I want his kisses.* "But I moved here without knowing him."

"We'll see...we'll see. Come on. Put the baby to bed and let's play!"

Thirty minutes later, Joey was down for the night. Both Romanos and Sophie had made themselves comfortable on the porch. "Keep the window open," said Mike.

Alison stood in the doorway. "You're welcome to listen, but you might be disappointed. This is a. . .hmm. . .let's call it a 'musicians at work' session. Not a polished performance."

"Maybe not today, but someday...and besides, my ears aren't what they used to be!" Paul Romano settled into the rocker and began to move it to and fro.

Alison smiled, by now understanding Paul's gentle humor.

"I was looking forward to this little concert," Paul continued, addressing Karen. "I knew you were the real deal 'cause Alison's the real deal, and in Pilgrim Cove, I've got connections."

Alison took pity on her friend's confusion. "The crowd at the pier saw you meet me with your fiddle. And let's just say that news travels quickly here."

They left the men and got their instruments. "Paul's like another grandpa for Joey and one of my unexpected summer listeners. I guess he doesn't want my little concerts to end."

Karen stared but said nothing for a moment. "Let's get started."

In no time, Alison plunged in, immersed in the music, stretching herself, but laughing at mistakes and quickly correcting them. Karen had brought music they'd tackled together in happier times. Ravel, Beethoven, Vivaldi—duets and sonatas for violin and cello. As naturally as breathing, Alison slipped back into her other role, totally focused, joyous until…Karen pointed her bow toward the ceiling.

"I think Joey's crying."

"Oh, my God, I didn't hear him." Alison jumped from her seat. "He usually sleeps through." Running to the baby's room, she scooped a tearful Joey from the crib. His hot little body told its own story.

"He's got a 101.3-degree temp," she said after reading the thermometer and returning with him to the kitchen. She dosed him with a baby aspirin. "He's drooling like crazy. Maybe he's getting new teeth."

"Probably."

"What's going on?" came a deep voice.

"Joey's sick. Hot. Maybe he's got a virus. Or strep throat. Or caught something from the kids at the library. Or he could be coming down with the flu."

Mike walked over and stroked Joey, still in his mom's arms. "Or maybe he's simply teething."

"That's what I think," Karen interjected. "My nieces and nephews always have something. Babies get fevers all the time."

"Joey doesn't. I guess he's been amazingly healthy, but I'm calling the pediatrician tomorrow."

"Absolutely," agreed Karen. "But for now…look, his eyes are closing again. I bet he's cooler and feeling better."

Alison nuzzled her son and agreed. She returned Joey to his bed, where he sighed and fell back to sleep. She sighed, too, and stepped to the doorway, where she almost tripped over the yellow lab. Sophie? Upstairs? The dog had positioned herself across the threshold. She wagged her tail, sweeping the floor with it, looked up at Alison, and whimpered.

"You, too? Not feeling well?" Ali patted the canine's neck. "Sweet girl," she whispered.

Back in the kitchen, she saw four cups of tea on the table.

"Decaf, I hope?" Glancing at Paul, she said, "You shouldn't have stayed outside all this time. It must be cold by now."

"Nah. The evening's perfect. It was Sophie who wanted in." He gazed up toward the bedrooms. "And now I know why."

"You do?"

"Yup. She sensed something not right with little Joey. He's part of her life now, so she's attuned to him."

"And I'm attuned to you," said Mike, staring hard at Alison. He glanced at Karen before settling on Alison again. "So what are you doing in Pilgrim Cove when you should be with your talented friend here in Symphony Hall?"

"My goodness, I've found an ally," said Karen. "You took the words right out of my mouth, but honestly, I didn't think you would."

"Joey and I like living right here," said Alison quietly.

"There are nannies, babysitters. Other women do it," protested Karen.

"Maybe. But I'm me. Not anyone else."

"And besides," continued Karen without pausing for breath, "doesn't that ferry run all year round?"

Her friend was a terrier holding on to her toy. "Can you picture my cello and me on a ferry?" She gazed through the window into the night, not meeting Karen's eyes. "Maybe...maybe...later on, I'll figure something out." She waved her arm at some distant future, hoping her friend would let the subject drop.

Instead, Karen took a deep breath. "Look. I wasn't going to say anything until tomorrow, but now that I've heard you again...oh, Alison, you're still so good! And there's another master class coming up that you can attend. You know how important they are."

Of course she knew. And if Peter hadn't died, she'd be the first one in line for the class. But that was then...

"I'm not ready..."

"You're going." Mike's no-nonsense voice. Insistent. Matter-of-fact. "Unlike me, you've still got the chops. Dad and I will babysit. You've worked for this all your life, now go chase the dream."

CHAPTER SEVEN

He'd lose her before he'd won her. Alison sat in the back of Mike's mind the entire next day. And in his heart. His divided heart. How could he not encourage her in what she loved? He wanted her to be happy. But at what cost to himself? *Kiss me again.* A spontaneous request from the woman he wanted to make love to forever. Alison Berg-Martin wanted him. He knew it, sensed it, basked in it. He also knew she'd want a full family life again one day. But that talent of hers! So special. He couldn't let her waste it. Slapping his own forehead, he knew if a man could drive himself crazy, he was the guy.

In the afternoon, he stopped by Sea View House to clean out the annuals. He could have sent someone else, but he needed physical action. Needed to move. Thank goodness his business required both mind and body.

He chatted with Joy MacKenzie, who'd been in residence since Rebecca had moved out. The vivacious kindergarten teacher lived up to her name. Always smiling. Always joyful, if a bit scattered. But she loved…no, adored…the garden he'd planted and could talk to him about each flower—if he let her. Today she seemed more effervescent than usual.

And then he noticed Logan Nash walking down the driveway, his Nikon on his hip. Little Bonnie and big Ajax, the German shepherd, trailed after him. The man had a gleam in his eye when he looked at Joy. His smile reached across the county.

So, that's the way of it. Mike's gaze traveled from one to the other, wondering if anyone else in their orbit had noticed. Or perhaps he noticed because of his feelings for Alison. Bart must be rubbing his hands in glee. Another match from Sea View House. He didn't utter a word, though, just shook hands with the other man, petted the dog, and stepped toward the child.

"Hi, Bonnie." He squatted to match her eye level. "How's school?"

"Fun! Miss Joy is my teacher. And Grandma's getting better."

"That's great. Give me five and then give Grandma five when you see her."

He pointed at the greenery. "Season's changing, Joy. We'll be raking and cleaning, wrapping some of the more delicate plants. You know, getting the place ready for winter."

"Perfect. But we'll need Halloween stuff…pumpkins and ghosts and witches….but first we're going to the apple orchard." Her gaze drifted somewhere only she could see. Logan rolled his eyes.

Mike nodded in mock commiseration. "We'll have everything you need at the garden center. Come on in anytime."

He eyed Logan's camera. The man was a pro, had covered the Mid East as a photojournalist. "Word's gotten around that you've been taking some local shots, on the beach and around town."

Logan nodded. "It's a friendly place."

"I was wondering," began Mike, "a friend of mine, a close friend, has a little boy. I can't think of a better gift…a surprise she'd really love…." He scratched his head. "Or maybe you just do…hmm…scenery and that kind of thing?" He hadn't been this tongue-tied since middle school.

"Oh, man. You've got it bad."

"Me?" *Buddy, you should see yourself.*

Logan slapped him on the shoulder. "I'm happy to help out with surprises. Just let me know when."

"Thanks. Thanks a lot." He left them, took a quick shower at home, and reported in for his weekly stint at the firehouse.

##

Alison had the coffee ready early the next morning when Mike pulled into his driveway. He waved and walked over.

"Thanks," he said, taking the mug.

"It's decaf. You need to sleep before heading to work."

He made a wry face. "Hate this stuff."

"Drink it anyway. It's hot." She cupped his cheek. "So, how was the night?" *Please say it was boring and uneventful and that it's always boring.*

"Lots going on," he replied. "Rescued one cat from a tree and made Mrs. Hargrove very happy."

Whew. She beamed at him. "I love that kind of night."

"While I can think of more exciting ways to spend an evening," he said, his words as slow and warm as a tropical breeze.

Heat burned her neck and face. She turned away, knowing her rosy skin now matched her hair.

He stepped closer and squeezed her arm. His forehead touched hers lightly. "Have a happy day, Red. Keep reaching for the brass ring. I'll have your back."

His words remained with her as she and Karen took Joey to the beach, searched for shells, and played ball on the sand. Her son's drooling had abated; he had no sign of fever and was his usual happy self. They ate lunch at the diner and began trekking several blocks to the local music store.

"I'll get the sheet music for the One Fund concert," said Alison, "and we can both play around with it later for a change of pace. I'll transpose for the cello, and you can read it as written."

"With a glass of wine, we'll have some fun."

Alison nodded. "I've got a bottle or two at the house. And…just to satisfy your curiosity…I'll tell you now. I've decided to register for the master class. Maybe it's time to get off the fence."

Karen stopped in her tracks. Her face lit with approval. "Bravo! You must have been tossing all night."

An image of Mike appeared, his calm blue eyes, sexy smile. *I'll have your back.* "Not really. I believe I have a bit of a support system."

"Oh-h…the support system," Karen teased. "And I like him. So, are there any more nice guys like Mike hanging out in this little town?"

"Maybe. But Sea View House offers the real action. From what I understand, men keep showing up at Sea View House thanks to Mr. Bartholomew Quinn, the Realtor who found this home for me. Now, *he's* a great guy, and if he were forty years younger…" She shook her head. "Sorry. I'm no help."

Karen brushed her words aside and pointed at the door ahead. "We're here. Let's go in."

"Come on, Joey. Out of the stroller."

They entered the shop, Alison searching for sheet music while Joey paused next to every instrument he saw. She kept watch on his travels, leaving her quest to be close by and name all the instruments for him. Proudly he pointed at the cello and preempted her. His eyes brightened at Karen as he named the "vi-lin."

Finally, Alison asked for sales help and downloaded copies of "Hero" and "Chariots of Fire" while Karen set Joey on her lap in front of a piano. "Piano. This is a piano."

"Pa-pa, Pa-pa. Papa plays piano."

Alison walked over. "Yes, he certainly does. I can't believe you remember."

He put his fingers on the keyboard and pushed one key at a time going up a scale. He cocked his head and grinned at his mom.

"Good job, sweetheart."

"I'm amazed he didn't bang on it like most kids do," whispered Karen.

"Play the Beethoven motif for him," said Alison. Karen obliged.

"More. More." Joey squeezed his hands under Karen's.

"Like this," she said, placing his fingers on the keys. "La, la, la…. .boom."

He sang the notes and let Karen play them with his fingers. Then he jumped down and ran to Alison.

"Mommy, Mommy. Joey plays piano." Such pleasure shone on his face, such excitement. As Alison watched him, memories returned. Little-girl memories. Herself. Her grandfather. And her dad. Making music.

She hadn't yet given much thought about Joey having natural gifts. Not with Peter's death, her son's birth, moving to Pilgrim Cove, and figuring out her own life. Which now seemed to be getting more complicated.

She jumped in surprise as music filled the store. Through a surround-sound system, she heard the four-note opening to Beethoven's Fifth. Joey ran from her, and as Alison watched in amazement, he lifted his arms and started "conducting." He continued through the entire first movement and banged his xylophone whenever the signature motif appeared. His smile never faded; joy radiated as he "worked" the music through both the dramatic and sweet tones.

Alison glanced at Karen, who was studying Joey as though he were a specimen in a Petri dish.

When the music stopped and quiet filled the store, Joey ran to Alison and wrapped his arms around her legs. "Good, good, good!" he exclaimed with excitement. She swooped him up.

"Beethoven's Fifth Symphony," she said, hugging him. "You just conducted the first movement of Beethoven's Fifth Symphony."

"Like it. Bay-to-ven. Joey like music."

She kissed him. "I know, baby. I know. And I like it, too. Good job. That was very, very good. You're a musician."

He nestled his head on her shoulder and took a deep breath. In seconds, his eyelids closed. "Joey play ball with Mike and Sophie," he whispered. A couple of deep breaths later, he slept, his body fully relaxed against her.

"He knocked himself out," joked Alison. "He must have been at it for over five minutes straight."

"Ma'am, the sonata movement runs eight minutes, fifty-one seconds." The store clerk came over. "We all enjoyed watching him. Especially since he didn't destroy the place. We have to watch out for kids, you know."

For the first time, Alison noticed other customers. Several smiled and whispered compliments about her adorable son. So cute. Like mother, like son. And on and on.

Karen opened the door and they left. "I'm thinking," Karen said, "that it's not just about you anymore. Is it?"

Alison looked away. Everyone had good intentions and ideas about what she should do. But she was the mother. In the end, it was up to her.

"Joey's not even two years old. I can provide him with all the musical opportunities he needs right here in Pilgrim Cove."

"Maybe for now," admitted Karen, "but not forever."

"I take it one day at a time."

##

She put up a strong front for Karen but couldn't wait to talk to Mike, who'd called before leaving work and would be bringing pizza for supper.

"If you're sure you want company?"

"Of course I'm sure. I want my friends to be…friendly. I'll provide salad, dessert, and wine."

"Beer's on me."

"Well, since I don't have any, bring some." She and Pete usually had a can or two of beer in the fridge. Seemed most men like having it around. "You and Paul come on over as soon as you can. It's been a rather…eventful day."

"Sounds interesting."

She hung up but wondered why she was eager to share her day with him, especially the part about Joey. Did she think he knew more about raising kids than she did? He didn't. But he cared about her son. Showed great patience. Made Joey laugh.

Alison couldn't miss the gleam in Mike's eyes when she opened the front door to the Romanos a few minutes later. It happened every time, and raised a warmth inside her that made her thoughts swirl.

"Hi," she said, staring as his mouth came down on hers. As naturally as breathing, she rose on tiptoe to respond fully. If he was surprised at her enthusiasm, it didn't show. He just whispered hello in a tone that spoke volumes more.

Soon the pizza boxes were in the recycle bin, and everyone adjourned to the living room, including Joey, in his pajamas, who climbed onto Mike's lap. Sophie lay on the floor next to them.

Alison gazed at the scene and sighed. "My new home is filled with friends. It's something I didn't know I'd want here, but maybe I just didn't know I'd need you all. It actually feels good."

Karen sat straighter, her gaze moving from Mike to Alison. "Which makes what I'm going to say even harder." She pointed at Alison. "You cannot stay in this little backwater town, sweetie. You've not only got to think about your own career, but now there's your precious son." She stepped closer and spoke softly. "You know how that's going to play out."

The woman crouched before the toddler. "You were amazing today, big boy, weren't you?" Turning toward the group, she filled Mike and Paul in on Joey's response to Beethoven's Fifth. Alison started to speak, but Karen cut her off.

"I've been through this with my nieces, and I'm saying that Joey is special. He's going to need special teachers. And this one"—she jerked her head toward Alison—"doesn't want to think about it." She smiled and waved nonchalantly at Mike. "Just thought you should know."

"And I think you should know," said Alison, "that if you weren't my closest friend, I'd send you packing. Right now."

She caught Paul's quick look at his son. The older man cleared his throat. "Does all this back-and-forth mean we're not getting a concert tonight?"

"Not to worry, Paul, if my friend," emphasized Alison, "remembers how to play her fiddle—"

"Ha! Some fiddle." Karen opened her violin case and produced her beautiful instrument. With a flourish, she played a few notes. "One more thing," she said, looking around the room. "Where in this house of music is the piano?"

Alison pictured her dad's baby grand in Boston. "Oh, come on, Karen. I can't afford a baby grand. I couldn't afford one with Peter, and I didn't need one."

Genuine surprise lit her friend's face. "Who said it had to be a baby? An upright is fine—for now."

"And so is a beginner's keyboard when he's ready." She looked at her son, who lay in Mike's lap, relaxed and content but alert to the exchange between the women.

"He's ready now," insisted Karen.

"Papa plays piano," said the boy. "Joey, too. Wash hands and play. Joey and Papa."

"Ahh…" from Karen. "Papa and grandson seem to have something going."

Really? "Next time we visit, you'll play with Papa again and have fun," said Alison, ignoring Karen's pointed comment.

Her son waved his hands and flexed all his fingers. But it was his sweet smile that tugged at her heart and made her smother him in kisses.

"You'll get a piano one day, sweetheart. In the meantime, how about sticking with your xylophone?"

She faced Mike. "I know you love music and are making mental notes, but rest assured, Joey doesn't need a piano quite yet. So let's pretend the subject was never brought up."

Walking toward her friend, she said, "And as for you...I'm a good mom. Trying my best. And it's not so easy. But one thing I've learned is this: bringing up a baby takes more than changing diapers, and it takes more than a piano. Have you ever wondered what else your sister is doing with her girls?"

Karen froze, then nodded. "Point taken. But...I've got you thinking." She began tuning her violin.

Mike let loose a long, low whistle. "You gals let it all out. No hiding behind a bunch of polite words." He pulled Alison toward him, kissed her lightly on the mouth. "You're a fantastic mom. And if this discussion had been about baseball, I'd weigh in. Right now, I don't know if Karen's a sinner or a saint with the hot buttons she's pushed. But *you* are the one in charge."

"Thanks," she whispered. His words rang true. She'd come a long way since her stay at Sea View House, since relocating to this house on Neptune Street, where she'd been going through the motions of living. She'd had a chance to catch her breath and was ready to move on. "Yes," she murmured. "I'm okay."

"'Atta girl. My money's on you." His raised brow and wide grin were contagious, and she found herself laughing with him.

Reaching for her cello, she sat down and glanced at the violinist. "How about giving my lovely neighbors something lovely to listen to?"

Karen smiled and raised her bow. "Of course. In the end, it's always about the music."

##

"I like the girl, son. I like her and the little one a lot, but it won't be an easy courtship." Paul sighed and patted Mike's shoulder. "You've had a couple of big losses already."

"So, what you're saying is that we're in the bottom of the ninth with bases loaded, two outs, and...I'm at bat." Mike met his dad's worried glance. "I've been in that spot before. Scary but exhilarating, too. And not impossible."

Ali was the sweetest, most courageous person. He loved that about her. He loved everything about her. Thank God she responded to his touch, his kiss. But she wasn't looking for a good time like the others he'd been with. The groupies hanging out at the field after a game, or hanging out in bars and clubs every night, looking...looking...for what? An uncomplicated one-night stand? A notch on their belt? Maybe they didn't know themselves. He never could figure it out, and now it didn't matter.

Alison thought he was a good guy, didn't she? But his grin was forced as he answered his dad's concerns.

"Alison's different from all the-the bimbos I've dated. I'm playing in the big leagues again, just a different game." He stroked his chin, scratched his head. "Maybe I just need a playbook."

"A playbook?" Paul asked. "Real love is not a game. Your mom and I... It was...not a game. It was wonderful and forever."

His dad rarely spoke so fervently about married life. And what did an active eleven-year-old boy know about the intricacies of marriage, even the relationship of his own parents?

"You still miss Mom." A statement, not a question. "That's a fact."

"You've been the best dad a boy could have. And that's a fact, too." Mike slung his arm around his father.

"Seems my job's not over yet," said Paul. "So what's this playbook gonna be about?"

"Hmm…I think you're right. Let's call it a plan. Alison's too important to be a game." Mike glanced at the time. Not too late. Reaching for the phone, he called Jason Parker. Busy or not, the musician would take calls from friends. And Mike would begin Step One of his plan.

CHAPTER EIGHT

Alison tossed, turned, paced, and traipsed to the
bathroom a dozen times that night. What if her friend
was right? Was she failing Joey because she'd chosen to
live in this "backwater" town? A town she now referred
to as home?

Although shaken at the relief of Karen's departure
late in the afternoon, Alison had hugged her friend and
urged another visit. The violinist's parting words stuck
in her head. "Register for the master class. Find a piano.
Move back to Boston." Karen needed a life of her
own! As she drove home, Ali had realized how full her
days had become since moving to Neptune Street. A
house, a child, a cello, and...Mike.

The phone rang as soon as she walked in the front
door. Jason Parker wanted to meet with her in his studio
Saturday afternoon with her cello.

"And definitely bring your little son. I want to
introduce you both to a couple of kids who know
something about music. Then you can decide if we're a
backwater town or not."

"Oh, boy. I know who mentioned that little idea to you, so don't defend him."

The man laughed. "This is too important to be only about Romano. Mike cares about you and your son. He wants what's best for both of you—and he didn't tell me to say that!"

She grinned. The famous musician sounded less than confident, but if what he said was true, then Mike had her back. "I guess I'm not the only parent challenged with a talented child...if that's what Joey is, which I can't say for sure."

"Sooner or later, he'll declare himself. Not deliberately, but naturally."

"Is that how you and Lila knew about your daughter? Her skills just showed up?"

"I'm afraid I wasn't around at the time, but Lila can tell you about it. She didn't miss a beat—no pun intended."

A story lingered behind his words, floating on the sound of regret. She'd never pry, but it seemed like Jason and Lila had had a rough beginning. On the other hand, it proved that circumstances didn't have to be perfect for a child to flourish.

"So, I guess I'll know when Joey lets me know." Which meant she had one less thing to worry about now.

"That's correct. In the meantime, we have an important concert in December, so I'll see you Saturday."

"Absolutely." She hung up and smiled at her son. "Come on Joey. Let's go outside and rake some leaves."

Joey raced to the door. "Rake leaves with Mike!"

"No, sweetheart. Mike's working. Rake leaves with Mommy."

He tilted his head back and bestowed a sweet smile. "Okay, Mommy. Go, go, go."

Mike showed up an hour later when she and Joey were sitting on the porch steps, taking a break. Her idea. Joey's engine was still running on a full tank.

"I could have sucked those guys up in no time with my riding mower," said Mike, eyeing the messy pile of leaves.

"No more favors, Mike." She looked toward her son. "We can do it, right, Joey?" But Joey's attention was elsewhere. He'd made a beeline to his big friend. A friend who lifted the child high and settled him on his broad shoulders.

"Ouch. Easy on the hair," Mike protested. "I've got you tight."

"Giddyap, giddyap." Mike took off at a trot, the toddler's squeals of joy filling the air.

A man and a boy. Alison watched them, heard their laughter, and a corner of her heart tore. This was how their lives—hers and Joey's—should have been. Pasting a smile on her face, she rose and took a step toward them just as a familiar black Lincoln pulled to the curb.

Bart Quinn.

The man got out and waved. "Just passing by and couldn't resist the pretty picture." He nodded toward the frolicking males. "Looking good, lassie, don't ya think? You brought the Sea View House magic right here to Neptune Street. You did, lass, indeed you did."

"Not a chance, Mr. Quinn. Sorry, but I don't believe in it." She had to admit, however, that her two "men" were having a great time together. She glanced at Quinn and read his mind. Not too difficult when a wide smile, a brief nod, and a blue-eyed twinkle were out in the open. To Bart Quinn, she, Joey, and Mike now seemed like a family. He didn't understand the difference between real and make-believe. Peter had been real.

"Have you ever lived in Sea View House yourself, Mr. Quinn?"

"No, darlin'. Sea View House was a private residence when I was a young buck. The gal for me lived right next door. My Rosemary…oh, she was pretty as a dream, and feisty, too. I didn't look anywhere else. Didn't need a Sea View House. But the young folks today…? Depending on a computer machine to meet a nice gal. What kind of romance is that? It can't compare to what happens at that special house on the beach."

A romantic to the bone, but he may have had a point. She noted, however, that neither he nor Paul Romano had ever remarried. Perhaps no one else measured up to their one true love. Would that be her story, too?

Mike's deep voice floated to her as he played with Joey. When he noticed Quinn, he took the child's hand and jogged over, matching his stride to the boy's. His warm gaze focused on Alison.

And her pulse picked up speed. Her heart seemed to race every time he showed up. His rich, deep laughter— so enticing—invited company. And she trusted him. But was she ready to move forward as he seemed to want? A month ago, she'd thought so. Sometimes, she was still unsure. The guilt was gone, yet Joey's dad would always be a part of their lives.

She had no time to muse further. Mike's arm came around her, and he pulled her close. She leaned into him, a comfortable fit.

"Way to go, boyo!" crowed Quinn. "You're putting roses in her cheeks."

He cocked his head, stared at Alison. "You brought the magic here, lass. The Sea View House Journal has another story on the way."

"And you've kissed the Blarney Stone too often," said Alison.

"She's got you there, Bart." Mike tilted his head and faced Alison. "But the stories he's talking about…are all true. I can vouch for Rebecca and my friend, Adam. You've met him—Sophie's vet."

"Of course. They seem very happy." Agreeable words, politely delivered. But magic houses didn't exist, and she wasn't Alice in Wonderland.

"More stories all the time," said Bart. "Now sweet Joy MacKenzie and Logan Nash are figuring it all out. With a little help from Ajax, that big war dog of his." Quinn rubbed his hands together. "I love a good plan. And that house on the beach, with its special rental arrangements, is the best one in Pilgrim Cove."

He punched Mike lightly on the shoulder. "And your little gal lived there, laddie. You're all set."

She'd appreciated sheltering there. The house had a sliding scale fee and a bunch of ROMEOs to check up on an overwhelmed young widow, a new mom with a six-month-old baby. A good place to start healing.

Mike rolled his eyes and opened the driver's-side door of the Town Car. "Time to get on home, Bart. Your good intentions are not helping." He checked his watch. "And I've got to run. I'm covering at the fire station tonight."

Alison's stomach tightened. She barely said good-bye to Quinn when he drove away. Scooping Joey into her arms, she faced Mike. "You already took a shift Wednesday night. You've done your time this week."

He stroked her forehead gently with his thumb. "That's better. No frown. Are you worrying about me, Red?" He tucked her close. "Not necessary."

And when the world crashes and a girl's blindsided…?

"One of the guys had to go out of town. A family thing."

Mike's business wasn't her business. He'd been part of the VFD for a long time, long before she showed up. "It's fine, Mike. Really. You just go do your thing."

She pulled away, muttering, "Everyone's got to be a hero."

"Look at me, sweetheart."

Sweetheart. She paused, glanced up.

"I'm nobody's hero." His soft voice rang with sincerity, each word measured. He reached for her hand. "I'm just an ordinary guy doing what I can for my hometown, for my friends and neighbors. Everyone does something."

"Not everyone."

He exhaled a deep breath. "You are so wrong. Who stepped in at the last minute for the temple congregation? Who gave her neighbors hours of listening pleasure as she practiced? And who," he whispered, "can set my heart on fire with a simple blink of her eyes?"

He leaned in, and his sweet kiss would have melted her if Joey hadn't chortled, "Me, too. Me, too. Up."

An aborted moment, rueful laughter. "See the complications I bring?" said Alison.

"He's a great kid. It's all about timing, and you're not scaring me."

"But you're scaring me," she whispered.

His brow rose, eyes widened, and a smile emerged. "Good. That's the plan."

Another night of little sleep.

She lay in bed, listening for the sound of sirens. When none came, she dozed, then jerked herself awake. She walked the house, peering through each window as if she had a view of the entire town. Which she didn't.

She was an idiot. Finally, in the small hours of morning, she allowed her herself to sink into her pillow and fall asleep.

When she next opened her eyes, Joey and his xylophone were in bed with her. She instantly became awake.

"Joey! How did you get here?"

He grinned, and her heart turned over. "You little monkey. Did you climb out of the crib?"

"Get up, Mommy, get up."

The clock radio said nine. No wonder Joey was raring to go…and soaked. "Come on, my man. New diaper time." She wasn't forcing the toilet training. According to the child-rearing books, boys trained later than girls, and it was pointless to nag until they were ready.

Joey ran into the bathroom and lay on the floor. "Change me."

"In here?"

"Mike here."

"No, he's not, silly. Mike's not here." Hopefully, Mike had gotten home and gone to bed.

She removed her son's wet disposable diaper and bagged it. Joey jumped to his feet, pulled his little stepstool to the bowl, and climbed up. "See, Mommy? Like Mike."

She saw, all right. When had Mike modeled male bathroom behavior? He'd never mentioned it. Shrugging, she smiled. Cute. And necessary. "Okay, Joe. What are you going to do now?"

And boom, he performed. And almost fell off the stool in surprise. "Ooh…" he said, "just like Mike."

"I'll have to take your word for it," she murmured before lifting him into her arms. "You are the best, Joey. The very best little boy. Let's try training pants."

He snuggled into her shoulder, humming the theme from *Chariots of Fire* perfectly in tune and on beat.

That afternoon, Alison drove to Jason Parker's recording studio on Main Street, almost at the Point, the very end of the peninsula. She didn't know exactly what to expect, but she didn't expect the size and high-end professionalism that met her eyes as he ushered her inside. The place boasted several performance areas, an acoustic control room, high-quality microphones, synthesizers, and mixers. In Pilgrim Cove, it was easy to forget that Jason Parker was a household name all across America. The piano man had made his mark at first by writing lyrics for others like pop star Luis Torres, then had started performing his own songs.

"Wow," she said, looking around. "I should have realized…"

"Welcome, welcome," he said, waving her inside and taking her tote bag. "Almost as heavy as mine. Who knew kids needed so much stuff just to go a few blocks?" He glanced at Joey, who was gazing around the room before starting for the piano.

"Congratulations on the new baby," said Alison. "Rosemary, isn't it?"

"Yeah, and thanks. The older kids will be here in a few minutes."

Mike had mentioned something about a big brouhaha between Jason and his agent out on the West Coast a few years ago. Jason wanted to relocate to his hometown; the agent was having fits. In the end, the musician had prevailed. "Jason was, after all, the talent," explained Mike with a sly grin.

It seemed the "talent" wanted to be with family and had chosen Pilgrim Cove.

Alison was the recognized talent in her little family. A talent with nowhere to go. And only God knew what surprises Joey might have up his little sleeve as time passed.

She set up her cello a short distance from the piano and then heard a myriad of excited voices behind her.

"Hi, Dad." A young girl carried a snare drum. "Auntie Laura dropped us off." She placed the drum on the floor.

"Hi, Uncle Jase." A two-boy chorus, the older child supporting a large backpack.

No question about the Parker kids being related— all shades of blonde and cute—not only in appearance but with a similar energy and eager smiles.

"Your daughter is Lila's image," said Alison while, from the corner of her eye, watching Joey find his way back to her with his xylophone.

"Lucky for her," replied Jason, ruffling the ten-year-old's hair. "How was the game, Katie?"

"We won, and Casey's team did, too. But not Brian's."

"We need another coach...I mean an extra one," said the older boy with a sigh. "Coach can't always make the practices."

Alison had a simple solution. "If you're talking baseball, why don't you ask Mike Romano? I think he knows something about the game."

The three youngsters stared at her, eyes as wide as dinner plates. "But he's a pro," whispered Casey. "He'd never do it."

"And besides," added Brian, "the season's over now. Football's started. And soccer. But next spring..." He turned to his uncle. "Whaddya think?"

Jason Parker met Alison's gaze and winked. "I think Ms. Alison might have some influence with the pro."

They looked at her with such awe she might have been a movie star. "I had no idea baseball was so important." From their admiration to disbelief in a nanosecond. "I mean, for musicians. Sports…and all." Lame. So lame.

"We don't worry about that," said Casey. "Uncle Jason says baseball never hurt him."

Before Alison could reply, she heard the first notes of "Take Me Out to the Ball Game" on the xylophone. She looked at Joey, who was sprawled on the floor. He turned his head and grinned. "Ball, baseball. Mike."

"Your son," said Jason Parker, with a raised eyebrow, "communicates very well."

Suddenly, in silent communication, the three Parker kids headed toward the piano. Brian grabbed a couple of music cases from his backpack. Alison recognized the violin shape and guessed at the square and oblong boxes. Flute, clarinet. She'd find out soon enough.

"Let's do a march," said Katie. "Babies like a march."

"Strong beat," agreed Casey.

An instant later, John Phillip Sousa's music filled the studio. Brian on flute, riffing in and out of the main theme of "Colonel Bogey" while four hands worked the keyboard. The two children stood side by side at the baby grand, sometimes changing positions between treble and bass without missing a note. Just having fun.

"Remarkable," whispered Alison. "Unbelievable." She glanced at Joey, who had run to the piano and was waving his arms to the beat like he had in the music store.

She glanced at Jason, but he had moved the drum toward her son and motioned him over. The man hit the drum softly with a stick and offered it to the toddler. "Want to try?"

Joey grabbed it. "Drum. Drum."

"But softly," said Jason. "Let's do it together."

As Alison watched, Jason soon let go of the stick, allowing Joey to continue alone. Her son kept time without a mishap until the children were finished. Katie and Casey ran over afterwards and sat on the floor with him.

"You were great, Joey. You didn't miss a beat."

"Yeah. You could play with us."

Joey looked at the children with adoring eyes. "Joey play. Joey play drums."

"He's not even two," Alison whispered as she watched the group.

"Sounds about right," said Jason. "You can't stop it. Whatever he's got in him will find a way out."

Her heart filled; her nerves tingled. She couldn't hide behind ignorance anymore. Her son had a gift, and it was up to her to provide him with an environment that nurtured it.

"I'll have to move…Karen was right."

"Why?"

"Well, you're the professional who could teach your kids, but Joey… I wouldn't know where to start."

He put out a hand, palm up to stop her. "Have you met Ellen Markowitz, the music teacher at Brian's middle school? She can play almost every orchestral instrument, and the kids love her. Do you know how many teachers would give their eye teeth to have a student like Joey? When he's a bit older, of course." He sighed. "Listen to me, from one parent to another, and leaving Mike out of the equation…"

With his sharp glance, she felt her cheeks flame at the mention of her neighbor.

"Maybe it's too late for that," Jason said with a laugh, "but I'm sure of one thing: stay here in Pilgrim Cove. Besides Ellen, there's the New England Conservatory Prep School. The ferry goes to Boston all year round, including Saturdays. Brian, Casey, and Katie are starting up again next week. When he's ready, your son will have all the lessons he can handle. The Conservatory starts them young."

She'd attended those Saturday classes herself while in high school, but she'd never wondered about the minimum age of acceptance.

Her mind raced. Jason had provided some answers, but the second one required money. Despite her excellent management of the household budget, she couldn't cover that expense at the moment. Maybe a job of some kind…? Private students? Well, she had time to figure it out.

"Thanks, Jason. The Prep School's a good option." She walked to her cello. "Now let's get on with what you really wanted us to accomplish."

"Good." He started pacing. "I want the survivors to walk out or wheel themselves on stage if possible and the cello to accompany them. You'll be stage right. We'll have big screens so everyone in the audience can see them up close and personal." He stared at her. "There'll be no singing, no chorus. Only the cello. The cello has to convey all the emotion the audience has in their hearts for these heroes."

Joey's issues would have to wait. Alison's mind raced to the images of that awful marathon day, to the profiles she'd read about the survivors, to her fellow Bostonians who'd come to the rescue. To Rebecca Fielding, right here in Pilgrim Cove, who'd lost a leg above the knee. Boston strong! Heroes all.

"Mommy tune cello."

She barely heard him. The musician had entered her own world. She picked up the bow and began.

CHAPTER NINE

She had coffee ready by the time Mike knocked on her door the next day.

"Mornin' glory," he said while bestowing a kiss.

"You're in a good mood," she said.

His wide grin made her laugh. "You blew Parker away. He couldn't stop talking about you, your emotionality, and Joey's potential. I swear he went on so long my ears started to hurt. He did mention Ellen Markowitz. I don't know her very well, but she's highly regarded in town. You should call her. At least you'd speak the same language, and she might be helpful with Joey-boy."

She nodded and smiled. "Jason and I had a good practice session. A medley of songs including the two we started with. More important…"

"You're staying in Pilgrim Cove," Mike interrupted. "That's what matters most."

She took a deep breath, squeezed his hand. "We'll have more time. You and I." She waited a moment. "I need that time, Mike, because things are happening fast for me now. Today my in-laws are visiting, and they're still grieving hard. And..."

"And you don't know what to say about me."

"Right," she whispered. "I didn't anticipate a new man in my life so soon. I can't add to their pain."

Mike started to pace the small kitchen. "It's been over two years now, Red. You're not giving them enough credit. They're presumably intelligent with life experience."

"But they lost a child. And nothing compares to that." Her gaze shifted to her son and paused there. "Can you imagine...?" she whispered.

"No!" His roar made her jump. Joey hid his face in her lap, and Mike's complexion turned pale.

"I think you understand now," said Alison as she patted Joey's back. "Shh...it's all right." Could Mike already love her son?

"It's okay, Joey, it's okay." Mike tousled the toddler's hair and kissed his forehead before meeting Ali's gaze. "Handle it any way you want. Maybe you can put that 'emotionality' to work. Just don't disappear on me." He leaned down and kissed her. "I won't compete with a dead hero, Alison. No living man can do that."

Her throat tightened to choking point. It hadn't crossed her mind that Mike would see Peter as competition. She grabbed his hand.

"I-I don't think it works that way. At least not for me." She chose her words carefully. "It's just a matter of fitting all the pieces together so that gaining you doesn't mean losing him."

Absolute silence followed. It mimicked the breathless silence after an outstanding performance on stage, the moment before the audience crashes back to earth and applauds like crazy. Alison's moment stretched. Even Joey remained quiet.

"You have a way with words," Mike finally whispered. "So we're a puzzle with a lot of pieces." He scratched his head. "And I thought I had a plan. A simple plan."

"Plans never work out," said Alison, "so save your energy."

"That's not true."

"Man plans and God laughs."

His brows rose. "As in, the best-laid plans of mice and men…?"

"Exactly. And I can attest to it."

"And that's why, darling, I've learned to make room for Plan B."

##

Or Plan C. No question that Alison had his heart. Just thinking about her brought a smile to Mike's face, as his dad had gleefully noticed on many occasions. He hadn't seen Paul as lighthearted in a long time. Not since Mike had been called up to the big leagues.

He glanced through his office window to the retail floor of the garden center. Paul was chatting away with customers, walking and pointing out possibilities. Still had a spring in his step.

"He can't really be retiring soon, can he, Soph?" He scratched the lab around her neck as she lay next to his desk and focused on the contracts lying on his desk. Tree trimming for the county, snowplowing for the town, and requests for bids on some commercial landscape projects to begin in the spring. He'd much rather be out with his dad and the guests, but Sunday was a good day to catch up on paperwork. Important paperwork that paid the bills and kept the Romano family in the black.

Sophie stood, whined, and trotted out to the store, tail wagging. The dog had a hundred favorite customers she liked to greet, and Mike went back to his computations—until he heard Joey's clear high pitch. "Sophie, Sophie! Wanna play?"

Mike rose and walked toward Alison and her family.

"Maybe we should get him a doggie."

The speaker had to be the mother-in-law. A trim brunette with a worry line on her forehead, her attention solely on her grandson, and her protective expression easy to read. She'd give him the moon if she could.

The look on Alison's face, however, made him laugh. A dog? Another responsibility? No chance of Joey getting a "doggie."

"Hi, Alison and…family. Welcome to the garden center." He smiled at them all and squatted down to Joey's level. "Sophie loves you, pal."

The child hugged the dog and beamed up at Mike. "We got a pumpkin. A big one."

"Great." He stood again. "You don't have to buy him a dog, ma'am. We live right across the street, and Joey plays with Sophie all the time." He'd use any opportunity to plant a seed with the grandparents.

Alison stepped forward and turned to her in-laws. "This is Mike Romano and over there"—she pointed to the adjacent aisle—"is his dad, Paul. They've been wonderful neighbors. Sophie is just the whipped cream on the top."

But the lady wasn't listening. "We could have bought you both a dog in Boston if that would have made you feel safer. You didn't have to move so far away. It took us almost two hours to drive here."

Alison darted a glance at him that clearly said, *See what I mean?*

"Hasn't Alison mentioned that we're only thirty minutes by ferry?" asked Mike. He smiled, aiming for a friendly, nonchalant conversation. "I commute for business regularly. Next time, you should give it a try."

Whew! The woman's eyes scorched him. She wasn't giving up her own agenda.

"Just a suggestion," Mike said quietly, "because I know Alison's door is always open to you. She wants Joey to know his grandparents."

Now Mr. Martin stared at him long and hard, his mouth tight. "You seem to know a lot about what our daughter-in-law wants," he said.

Mike slipped his hands in his pockets and shrugged. "If I do," he said, keeping his voice low and even, "it's because we've become friends as well as neighbors." He stepped back. "Work's waiting," he said, ready to return to his office. "Great to meet you. And here comes my dad. Alison can introduce you."

He'd leave it to his friendly, people-oriented dad to calm the couple down and disarm them. Mike had accomplished his goal by planting that seed. He and Alison were friends. Her in-laws needed to realize Alison was not living in an isolated castle surrounded by a moat, but he knew they resented his intrusion. To them, his friendship spoiled the image they had of Alison as their grieving daughter-in-law.

But time didn't stand still, even for a young widow. He whistled a cheerful tune and got to work on the project that excited him. The garden center's first-ever brand-new greenhouse. Who would have thought when he'd been cut from the pros almost two years ago that running a business, building a greenhouse, and meeting an exciting woman could replace the ache of that disappointment?

He'd had choices back then, but they'd boiled down to one: *live or die*.

He certainly hadn't planned to fall in love. He'd just wanted to lend Red a helping hand like he did with the residents of Sea View House. But those best-laid plans...? To his surprise, he'd watched an amazing woman slowly emerge from her cocoon, trying her new wings, creating a new path, and drawing him closer to her. And somehow while the groupies had followed his team, he'd stopped trying to prove himself as a player after the sun went down. After meeting Alison, he'd never looked back at the clubs and women.

Now she had the same decision he once had: *live or die.*

He forced himself to be patient and give her space. She was stronger than she realized, but that new path she was carving was still in shadow. If she asked, he'd help clear those shadows away, but he wouldn't coax or browbeat. For Alison to be happy again, she needed to believe in herself, in her own strength.

For Alison and him to have a future together, they had to meet as equals.

Heck, he didn't even have all the answers! He was just going with his gut. Bart would be proud.

##

Pale rays of sunlight lingered on the beach at the end of the fall day. The breeze off the Atlantic made Alison put sweatshirts on Joey and herself while Mike stayed in his short-sleeve jersey. The steady rhythm of the waves rushing to shore provided a comforting background.

"Of course Dad and I can babysit Joey! You're not missing that master class." Seemed Mike didn't get the message about the comforting tide.

Her parents had a conflict next Saturday and couldn't babysit, so she'd asked Mike. Now, however, she had second thoughts.

"I'll be away most of the day…and…"

"And we'll be fine," said Mike. "Joey loves the garden center, and between Dad and me, we'll figure it out."

"Puh-lease. If it weren't for Sophie, I'd be more worried."

"Is that right?" His eyes flashed with amusement, and he stepped toward her in mock threat.

Alison took off running. Free as a gull, she flew across the sand, not pausing, not worrying about anything. Only a stitch in her side slowed her down after awhile. She lifted her arms and whirled in place on this perfect evening. From her starting point, Mike and Joey jogged at a snail's pace until Mike lifted the little guy for a piggyback and increased his speed.

Alison started toward them, surprised at the joy running through her. A reawakening after a long sleep.

"Do you know how beautiful you are?" asked Mike softly while putting Joey down.

"Huh?" She looked closely. His gaze caressed her, his arms encircled her waist, and she floated toward him.

"Let me show you how beautiful," he whispered.

His mouth met hers with a soft touch, slow, thoughtful, and his tongue traced the outline of her lips, then the recesses of her mouth. She leaned in, took a breath, and inhaled his male scent mixed with the sea breeze. A wonderful combination.

"Hmm…more…"

"Yes, ma'am."

His lips covered hers again, and this time the kiss hardened. She grasped his broad shoulders, muscles firm beneath her hands, and nestled closer against his body. He gasped.

"My God, you're incredible," he murmured between kisses, "but we have an audience." He backed up, kept holding her hands, and lifted them to his mouth. His steady glance captured her. "I am more than ready, sweetheart, whenever you are. And I hope it's soon!"

She understood his meaning exactly and had to acknowledge it. "You're pretty incredible yourself."

"Don't embarrass me, Red. You add so many new facets and enrich my life, yet you make it easier, too."

She caressed his cheek. "That's saying quite a lot since all I've ever done is cause you more work."

His cheeks became ruddy. "Fugeddaboutit!"

That evening, with a light heart, she picked up her bow and began looking forward to the master class, the class Mike made happen for her with his offer of day care. Amazing.

Her mind settled as she went through the familiar ritual of tuning the strings and practicing scales. She and the others had been assigned specific pieces to prepare in advance, each one different. She'd perform the first thirty-two measures of Verdi's *Aida*, and participate in a Brahms piano trio with a violin and herself on cello. Afterward—the critiques. An excellent means for developing musically.

But to what end except for her own pleasure? After warming up, she erased the problem from her mind and concentrated on Verdi and Brahms. Within minutes, she had no problems other than the challenges of the music.

Untold times in the past, she'd considered herself the luckiest girl on earth to spend her time with glorious masters—the brilliant Mozart, beautiful Verdi, and lyrical Brahms. Their music had filled her heart. She couldn't imagine being more fulfilled.

Until she'd fallen in love with Peter. And Joey. And now it seemed that heart of hers was embracing another love. Unlooked for. Unwanted. Yet…the friendship worked.

On Saturday morning, Joey kissed her bye-bye and bounded out the door with Sophie. Mike was right behind them. Through the window, she saw Mike bend down and whisper something in Joey's ear. Her son looked up and waved, all five little fingers flexing. She watched Mike bundle her son into the backseat of the garden center's long-bed truck, a truck loaded with toys, pull-ups, extra clothes, diapers, too, and the xylophone. No crying, no looking backwards, Joey was off to an adventure with people he trusted. Her lips trembled as she acknowledged the first time she and Joey would be separated by many miles—and waved as Mike's truck pulled away.

Catching her breath, she returned inside, grabbed her cello and car keys, stuffed the sheet music in her tote along with her purse, and headed toward the pier. In five minutes, all thoughts of Joey fled. Boston awaited. Her other life waited. Her body tingled with a mix of excitement and anxiety, but she was ready for this. She needed to test herself. More than that, she *wanted* to revisit her professional life. How else could she plan for the future? Her future. Joey's future. That ordinary word now seemed extraordinary with its big-picture ideas. So much bigger than getting through one day at a time, hiding in the house.

She wasn't alone on the pier, but was always surprised that using a boat was considered "normal" transportation. Lou and Pearl Goodman smiled and stepped closer, and soon she was surrounded by members of the ROMEO group. Bart Quinn stood a few yards away, talking to a tall, striking woman Alison didn't know. As she watched, the woman threw her head back and laughed with hearty amusement, the sound rich and full. Her long earrings sparkled in the morning sun. A suitcase rested on the ground nearby.

"Is that his sister?" Alison asked. "She's got the same high energy."

"Bart has no sister," said Lou. "I have no idea who that lady is, but I bet we'll all know within five minutes. He's been talking to her since she debarked from the earlier ferry."

"We missed that one, so he waited for us," said Pearl, eyeing the cello. "We have another concert today at Symphony Hall. Are you, by any chance…?"

Alison understood the woman's unspoken question. "No, no…I've never auditioned for the Boston Symphony." Just when she'd felt ready and had begun tracking blind auditions, her world had collapsed. "I was a member of the South Shore Philharmonic and loved it. But today, I'm off to a master class." She glanced at their whole group. "You guys don't miss out on anything, do you?"

"No, we don't, young lady. After the concert, we treat ourselves to dinner in a good restaurant." The speaker was an older version of Jason Parker, same mane of wavy hair, but would definitely be described as salt and pepper, heavy on the salt.

"You must be…" began Alison.

He extended his hand. "I'm Sam Parker, from the hardware store. Jason was telling me about you and your boy. I never worried about teachers, just taught my boys all I knew, and they went on from there." He glanced at his hands. "A little too much arthritis now, but I can still play a note or two."

Another resource for her. She'd bet the man could play a heck of a lot more than a note or two. The ferry's horn sounded from the near distance. They had a few minutes before boarding.

"Ahoy, everybody." Bart and his new friend joined them. "I'd like to introduce a first-time visitor to Pilgrim Cove. This is Joy MacKenzie's aunt Honey. And she's been stranded at the pier." His blue eyes gleamed, but the woman's did, too.

"A good storyteller," she said, glancing from Bart to her watch. "I'm sure my sister will be here in a minute. We're all getting together at Joy's place."

"Never mind your sister," said Bart. "I'll be happy to bring you to Sea View House myself. In style, too."

His Lincoln Town Car. Over ten years old, but the man was crazy about it. Alison glanced at the others, who'd known Bart for decades. If she only had a camera… The group's collective jaw had dropped, their eyes frozen wide in disbelief before they regained their composure and greeted the new arrival.

"Everyone loves Joy," said Marsha Rosen. "The best kindergarten teacher ever."

"And so creative," added Pearl. "A real artist in everything she does, even sand sculptures." She smiled at the woman. "You should have been here during Labor Day weekend when the annual contest takes place. Ask her about it."

Honey beamed and clapped her hands together. "I'm her favorite auntie, you know. We're on the same wavelength." She glanced at her suitcase. "I've closed my art gallery for the season and am heading to Florida. It's time to buy a condo. I've had enough New England winters to last a lifetime!"

"Florida?" boomed Bart. "You'd leave your family?"

"Not till after Christmas," she replied. "And my family is perfectly capable of surviving without me for a few months. In fact, they can hop on a plane and visit."

Bart picked up the woman's suitcase. "We can talk about that on our way."

Alison watched the two leave the dock. "He's going to miss the concert," she said absently.

"Good God," said Lou. "I think the man's smitten."

"She's a beautiful woman," said his wife. "Stunning, actually, and no shrinking violet. It'll be a sparring match for sure."

Small-town life was never dull. Alison boarded the ferry along with the ROMEO crowd and others, her mind refocusing on her class. Bart Quinn's life was his own to manage. So was everyone else's. Each path was sometimes smooth, sometimes rough, but always held choices. She reached for the music score and began reviewing it in her mind. The bowing, the phrasing, the overall shape.

She was so lost in concentration she gasped when Rowes Wharf came into view. The Boston Harbor Hotel, the Harborwalk, the restaurants. She returned the music to her bag, took a deep breath, and clutched her cello with both hands. She was as ready as she'd ever be.

The first person Alison saw in the rehearsal hall was the conductor of the South Shore Philharmonic. Her surprise was an understatement. She was shocked and almost allowed the cello to slip from her hands.

Maestro Bekker's greeting was warm, generous. "I knew you'd be back," he said. "A little time to adjust was all you needed." He smiled and nodded. "That's why I approved your application for this workshop."

"I had no idea," whispered Alison. "Karen nagged and nagged, and I just didn't think about it. Of course, it makes sense. The classes are open only to working musicians or students."

"Better that way," said the maestro. "Now let's see how the day goes."

Two dozen music students and professionals filled the chairs in the open workshop, wanting to hear and learn from the best. The best included not only Maestro Bekker but top cellist from England Richard Jenkinson, who was performing a series of concerts in America.

Three hours flew by.

"More depth...don't ice-skate across the piece..."

"The music! The music is in the spotlight...not you..."

"The instrument is your voice...speak through it...."

Details of attack, tone, and phrasing of the piece were all part of a master class.

Alison soaked in every minute of work, beauty, and technical corrections. She reconnected to happiness. Her first joy. If she had wings, she would have soared. This... *This* was what she was meant to do with her life. Her professional life. And she'd earn a salary, which she needed. Could she teach instead? Sure. Did she want to? Not really.

All this time, while she was running from her remorse and other fears, she'd run from her career. One truth slammed her in the gut now: she couldn't hide forever.

The maestro approached. "When are you returning? I will make a spot for you in the string section."

Now her heart thumped with a heavy beat. Committing to the orchestra required two rehearsals a week plus concerts and practice, and she'd be getting paid for doing something she loved. She pictured Mike's gleaming eyes and wide grin and wanted to grin back. He'd cheer for her. Michael, Michael. Mike Romano was a critical part of her life. Joey's life. Morning coffee, evening kiss, and everything in between.

She wanted it all.

Pressing the conductor's hand, she said, "I'll be in touch. I-I need to figure it out."

CHAPTER TEN

"No guts, no glory." Mike pulled Alison closer to him and kissed her on the mouth. "Have I mentioned how proud I am of you?"

"Only about a thousand times. And thank you." She smiled and kissed him again. And had to admit, the invitation to rejoin the orchestra had brought her close to tears, happy tears, that afternoon. She still had it—joy, sensitivities, and skills—and she credited her nightly practice sessions with her wonderful instrument, almost a living, breathing thing to her.

"Oh, Lord. That mouth, your smile…do you even know what that smile does to me?"

Well, she had some idea.

"Never mind," said Mike. "We'll get back to that later. So why are you hesitating about going back to the orchestra? It's like a second chance at the majors. I don't understand."

Alison glanced toward Joey's bedroom. The baby was sound asleep after his busy day exploring Mike's store. Sophie was across the street with Paul. According to Mike, the big dog had proven her maternal mettle and would sleep well after herding her little charge.

"Gotcha," said Mike, who'd intercepted her glance. "It's Joey. If you're worried about your son, don't. Dad, Sophie, and I can watch him again when you need to rehearse."

He was so sweet, so loving, she felt tears well and spill over. Rubbing her eyes with one hand, she caressed his cheek with the other. He took it, kissed it, and said, "Talk to me."

"You are wonderful to offer, but"—she shook her head—"you don't understand the commitment… If my parents lived here…or even my in-laws…"

"Forget them." He put his hand under her chin and raised it until her eyes locked with his. "I understand commitment very well. And promises. And responsibility. So think about this: what would you have done after Joey's birth if Peter had lived?"

Her head jerked back; her mouth fell open. "How can you ask that? Peter would have pitched in. He was my husband!"

"A man who held a full-time responsible job with crazy hours. And as for your folks, they're not yet ROMEO material and are still working full-time. So, what would you have done? Quit the orchestra?"

Her mind raced, her thoughts running in circles. She stepped back, covered her mouth. "I-I don't know. I really don't know. Pete-Peter… He-he never even knew about Joey." Tears welled again, not from long-held guilt this time but from sorrow.

She heard Mike's inhalation. His long, "Oh-h, baby…" And felt his arms around her, his embrace gentle and protective.

"That's quite a burden you've carried…must be a huge regrct…"

"For a long time," she whispered, "I tried to rewrite the ending. Grieving him was hard enough, but remorse and regret were killing me. I'm trying to let it go."

"Since you can't change that ending," Mike said slowly, "perhaps it's time to write a new beginning."

Quiet surrounded them as she absorbed his words. His intent was clear, but she wasn't ready. And maybe he picked up on that.

"You can start with figuring out the orchestra," he said. "Basically, there's no difference between then and now. You have a child and a career."

Maybe he was right. She'd postponed reality for as long as she could. "I need a job. I definitely need a job. Insurance won't last forever."

He reached for her, held her close. "You need a hug, a kiss…"

As long as that hug and kiss came from Mike Romano. Raising herself on her tiptoes, she wrapped her arms around his neck. "You're a wonderful listener," she whispered. "You've had my back since I moved here, and I don't know why."

He laughed softly and continued to hold her. "I hope you'll ask me again in fifty years."

Fifty years? She held herself tight, but her knees shook. Talk about commitments. He couldn't have made himself clearer. "You're on a faster track than I am, Mike Romano."

"Not a problem," he said, kissing her quickly. "I have total confidence you'll catch up very soon."

##

She wasn't the only woman in the world who had to consider day care for her child. That's what Alison told herself as she began making phone calls. To Lila Parker, whose baby was now five months old, to her pediatrician for referrals, and finally she spoke to some of the other mothers at the library.

"I'll be happy to watch him myself in an emergency," said one. "Our kids play well together."

"Thanks," said Alison. "But I really need a commitment for two days a week. But you'll be my official emergency backup. And of course, I'd pay you."

And that meant she wouldn't have to bother Mike, who had a business to run.

"Call Tiny Treasures," someone else suggested. "I hear good things, and they're licensed."

"Lila Parker already suggested that, so I made an appointment and visited. Joey's on a long waiting list, no openings in his age group until January."

And that's what she explained to Mike late that evening after her practice session. He'd let himself into the house and stretched out on the couch, listening. Probably dozing, too. But afterward, as she sat with him on the sofa, she filled him in.

"As long as Maestro Bekker knows my intentions, he can plan. I can't make promises I might not be able to keep."

He pulled her down against him. "I can handle little Joe for two months or so."

She shushed him with gentle fingers across his mouth and sat up again. "I know you could, but it's really not an ideal arrangement for both your sakes. He needs child activities, and you need your mind on the garden center. Halloween's almost here, and then the big holiday season. I know how busy you are."

He sighed, a sound full of disappointment, which hurt Alison's heart. She squeezed Mike's hand.

"I've got to do this myself."

"Why?"

"To prove to myself that I can stand on my own— without hiding in the house."

He sat up and swung his legs to the floor. His arm came around her. "Oh, baby, you've come a long way since then. And you're not alone anymore."

But she was. She had to keep some distance between them. "You're at risk every week on that fire truck. There are no guarantees about anything."

His kiss was gentle, and when he spoke, his voice was gentle, too. "Not true. I can guarantee my love for you. Today. Tomorrow. Always."

Her breath hitched. She hadn't had luck with a*lways.*

"I love you, Red." He pointed at the cello. "That beautiful music you play…that's my heart talking to you. And I hope you're not afraid to answer."

He deserved an answer. But she couldn't say everything he wanted to hear. She cupped his face. "Michael, Michael, you're so easy to love. I'm vulnerable with you, really, I am. But that fifty-year timeline you mentioned the other day…? We joked about it, but you deserve an honest response." She took a deep breath. "I don't know if I'll ever be in for the long haul. It's very risky… terrible things can happen." She took a breath. "And I-I'm sorry. So very sorry."

His face became a blank mask, and he rubbed his chest. "Then I suppose," he said, his tone quiet but steady, "I'll have to have faith for the both of us."

##

Sleep eluded her that night. Peter's and Mike's images swirled in her mind. She'd loved Peter "until death did they part," but her feelings for him were different from her feelings for Mike. With Peter, she'd jumped into the deep end, full of confidence and joy. The future had been theirs with no thought of adversity. She was different now. Older, with heart-wrenching experience, and maybe that was the reason for the blinking caution lights that accompanied her thoughts of Mike.

Mike Romano could make her laugh and cry, he could stir her to anger and embarrassment, and could bring her to her knees with his kindnesses. When he appeared at her door, her heart picked up speed. No question that her feelings for him were intense. But was it love? Or was she simply a coward, afraid to love again? She punched her pillow, lay down, and closed her eyes. Her thoughts kept her company until she fell into a restless sleep.

When pale sunlight crept through the cracks of her blinds, she quickly rose from her bed. Walking softly, she went to her computer as she always did at the start of her day. Email first. All the parents wanted another visit. Karen wanted to know when to expect her at rehearsal. Fliers from department stores offered percentage-off sales. Ellen Markowitz, the music teacher, was confirming their after-school date that day. And the Conservatory Prep School had sent her information about older pianos now for sale to the public.

She checked her calendar next, surprised to note how it was filling up. Joey was now part of a playgroup each Tuesday morning with some of his library friends—her friends, too. She had an appointment at the Wayside Inn that morning, prompted by their unexpected phone call earlier in the week. Would she like to provide the ceremonial music for an upcoming wedding? She'd be paid well.

She tapped her fingers on the kitchen table, knowing she'd accept that assignment and any other that came her way. Extra earnings could be put toward the piano without dipping into savings. Maybe she should print up business cards...? Was she a real business? She'd ask Mike for an opinion.

After brewing coffee, she went onto the front porch to wait for him. After ten minutes, she called his house and spoke with his dad.

"Mike's already at work. Must have had a big project on his mind."

"Oh?" Her heart began to thud. "He didn't mention it. So, I've got a full pot of coffee here. Want a cup?"

"A shame to let it go to waste. I'll be over."

She slowly placed the receiver in its cradle. A big project? Mike always had a myriad of projects to oversee at the design center but had never turned down his morning joe before. Seemed he'd slept as poorly as she had last night. Which meant the big project on his mind might have been her.

Returning to her computer, she sent him a note: *How about dinner tonight? My house. Bring your dad, too.*

His reply came an hour later. *The Lobster Pot. 6:00. I'll pick you up. Give Joey a nap today.*

##

She signed a four-hundred-dollar contract with the Wayside Inn for the wedding. The couple wanted the cello not only for the ceremony—the processional and recessional marches—but the cocktail hour preceding it. A two-hour gig. Plus time to polish the Wagner and Mendelsohn pieces and her own selection of classical and pops music, all time spent at home.

"Your name has gotten around," said the manager, leaning toward her over his desk. "The ROMEOs, you know, never keep good news to themselves. And when Jason Parker vouched for you…well, what more needs to be said?" The guy looked so happy she wanted to laugh.

Instead, she shook his hand, a bit overwhelmed but thankful for the praise from her new friends as well as the man's enthusiasm. She wasn't too overwhelmed, however, to ask if he'd keep her in mind in the future. With a few engagements right here in town, she'd be able to get that piano.

"C'mon, Joey. Time for lunch." And a nap. Tricky business with the growing toddler who fought naps during the day.

In the end, it was the music teacher's violin and Alison's cello that soothed Joey to sleep in the afternoon.

"We must be very good," quipped Ellen, "to knock him out so fast."

"He's used to me playing at night. Maybe he's been conditioned." Alison grinned. "Anyway, I'm so glad to finally meet you."

"I feel the same. It's wonderful having another pro in town, someone who actually knows what pizzicato means—without me having to explain it!" The woman seemed totally relaxed. Older than Alison, Ellen was married with two children. Her husband taught math in the high school.

"I'm glad the kids are getting a good musical education," said Alison, nodding her head. "You seem to have lots of energy and patience."

"The children are great. Music's an elective, remember, so the students I teach want to be there. No one's forcing them. It's hard reining them in sometimes, but it's such fun, too. And so rewarding. I love it. Love what I'm doing." She leaned in. "Of course, I'm always afraid the budget will shut the program down, but so far, it never has."

"That would be awful."

"I've got some talented kids in my classes in addition to Brian Parker, who's in a class by himself.

The others deserve attention, too, but I don't give private lessons." She shook her head. "No time. I've got my own family to take care of."

"Of course. And you need time to practice and play."

"I grab an hour whenever I can."

One tiny hour didn't sound like much to Alison, but she nodded and tried to smile.

"Just look at your face!" Ellen grinned. "You think I'm a slacker, don't you?"

"Oh, no," said Alison quickly. "You have so many other responsibilities....your family and classes. I guess our goals are different."

Ellen's smile faltered. "I'm not sure about that. Isn't the goal for music to enrich our lives and make us happier? There's more than one path to achieve that, and we've simply chosen different ways."

Alison studied her new friend, who seemed to have figured out what Alison was still struggling with. "You are a wise woman. I'm glad we found each other."

Funny how Karen's joy in music was laser focused on a solo career while Ellen's blended in with her family and friends. Nothing was black or white, right or wrong. The choices of these musicians were as individual as the people behind them. Alison saw that more clearly now.

As for herself, she needed to make all the pieces of her life fit together and claim her spot on the happiness scale. Simple.

##

Fear made her commitment-phobic. That's what Mike told himself while he shaved that evening before getting Alison and Joey. It wasn't personal. She loved him. He told himself that, too. Her kisses were too sweet and her body language too trusting not to love him. He knew the difference, considering all the women he'd been with a lifetime ago. If he'd accepted Alison's invitation for dinner at home, they might easily have wound up in bed. He could barely keep his hands off her, but that wasn't how he wanted to win her over. So the safest way to spend time together was in public. Besides, they'd all have a fabulous meal, to boot.

When she opened the door, all noble thoughts fled. "You look beautiful," he said. Dangling earrings, a green fitted sweater, and long black skirt. And when she smiled, he wanted to pull her close and kiss her until she begged him to stop. His hands twitched, and with effort, he managed to control himself.

"I guess I clean up pretty well when I have the time." She opened the door wider. "Come on in. I'm packing Joey's carry bag."

"Mike! Mike! Mike!" Joey wasted no time running at him. He caught the boy and lifted him.

"You look clean and handsome, Joey," he teased. "Ready to go out?"

"Rest-a-ront. Hot dog!" He looked around. "No Sophie. Mommy said."

"She's right. But guess what?"

"What?"

"I think you'll see the kids. Casey, Katie, and Brian."

Without hesitation, Joey began singing the tune of the "Colonel Bogey March." Mike joined in. Alison contributed her soprano while he led them to his personal SUV, where Paul waited in the gathering dusk.

"But my car's got the car seat," said Alison, pointing to her sedan in the driveway.

"So does mine."

Her eyes widened. "Really?"

Opening the rear door, he placed Joey inside and buckled the belts. "I bought it awhile ago. How else can I bring the little guy along with me?"

"Point taken…I guess," she said, looking confused. "They're expensive."

"Better safe than sorry," he countered. "Besides, I got a good price online. It's the same one as yours."

She squeezed his arm. "You're really incredible."

Score one for him. But he'd play it cool now. "Dad, you want the front or the back? It's a family outing. Not a date. The choice is yours."

Paul opened the back door. "Hey, Joey. Long time no see."

Alison's mouth formed a perfect circle. "Family outing?" she mouthed.

He shrugged. Maybe he wasn't so cool. "Whatever."

##

Lanterns hung from the roof of the Lobster Pot's spacious wraparound porch, where, in summer, many diners gathered to enjoy their meal. No outdoor tables now, but the warm lights welcomed them out of the chill of mid-October. More important, a smiling Maggie Sullivan, partner with her sister in the restaurant and also Bart's daughter, was at the door to greet them.

"We're so happy to see you again," she said to Alison. "It's tough getting out with such a little one." She kneeled to Joey's level. "Guess what? Katie and Casey are waiting for you. They need a drummer." She rose and winked at the adults. "Follow me. We're all in the main dining room."

"All?" asked Alison, picking Joey up so he could see better.

Maggie chuckled. "When my dad's around, he wants all his 'peeps' with him!"

"There's no table big enough for that," replied Paul. "Bart Quinn knows every man, woman, and child in the town."

The woman paused in her stride and turned to face them. "It seems there's one woman who managed to get away. And he's not liking it."

"Away...as in Florida?" asked Alison as memories of her encounter on the pier rushed back.

"Oh, yeah. As Dad says, 'Honeybelle's got him in a tizzy.' It's unbelievable after all these years."

"My, oh, my," said Paul. "The mighty are taking a tumble."

"More like a hard fall." Maggie inclined her head and led the way through a central aisle toward the main dining room, where two tables for twelve—already half-occupied—waited.

She led them directly to the table with Jason and Lila, Matt and Laura, and all the kids, including Baby Rosemary. "It's our usual Friday night family get-together sometimes followed by my dad's hot poker game. Don't know his plans tonight, though."

Joey bounced in Alison's arms as soon as he spotted the children. "Ka-tie, Cas-ey, big boy, big boy."

"That's you, Brian," said Mike, taking Joey from his mom. "You're his big hero."

With a moment's rearranging, everyone found a seat. Maggie's sister, Thea, came over to chat. "We're so happy you've found time to visit. Another musician in Pilgrim Cove is so great. You're all I've heard about for the past two weeks. Welcome."

"Thank you. Thanks so much." Alison looked around the cheerful restaurant. "I was here only once before, and that was to pick up a to-go order. I never really saw the place."

Mike chuckled. "You're in for a treat. Take a look." He pointed at colorful signs on the wall, all with a nautical theme. "They're full of puns. Some good, some not so much."

He pointed to an impressively large sign with sea creatures around the edges. In the middle, however, it boasted in big, bold letters: *The Lobster Pot—Where No Lobster is a Shrimp!"*

"I like that one. It works."

She grinned. "Very punny. Who comes up with these things?"

"The sisters—Maggie and Thea. They like seeing the town on their walls. Look over there. A bit of romance."

Alison studied a cartoon of… "Oh, my. That's Laura and Matt Parker." The caricature of Matt had him wearing an oversized tool belt and holding a wrench up over his head with Laura sitting balanced on top. His other hand was fisted on his hip. He winked at the viewer. The slogan said: *Matt Parker loves his wench!*

"He and his dad run the hardware store…" began Mike.

"I get it, I get it. It's a lot of fun." She slowly scanned the other posters and jumped when Bart's voice surprised her.

"There's a common denominator, you know," he said, his blue eyes twinkling as a smile hovered around his mouth. "Sea View House! Just look. There's Professor Daniel Stone and Shelley Anderson Stone."

Alison saw a pretty beach scene with the professor in a mortarboard hat and tassel, dragging a wide-tooth rake through the sand. The caption read: *Professor Dan combed the beach till he found the perfect Shell-ey!*

"Aww," she managed. "Very sweet."

"They're summer folks," said Bart. "Live in Boston and spend lots of weekends and all summer with us. I helped them find the perfect place."

"You have a million stories, Bart, don't you?" asked Alison.

The old man's gaze went from Alison to Mike and back again before he answered. "That I do, lassie, but they're all in the Sea View House Journal. You'll read it one day and enter your own story, my dear. Right after Joy MacKenzie and Logan Nash write theirs."

"Oh-h…I don't—"

"The Sea View House magic is with you, lassie. A part of you." He turned to Mike. "And don't you mess it up!"

"Me?" His chin jutted out, and a calculating grin crossed his face. "I hear a certain Ms. Honeybelle's got *you* in a tizzy. So, what are you going to do about it?"

A sudden silence fell over the crowd. Mike had provoked the town's favorite son with *the topic* of the day. All ears tuned in.

"Young man," said Bart, reaching for the inside pocket of his jacket, "you haven't stumped me." He pulled out an envelope and waved it. "Here's my boarding pass. I'm off to Florida tomorrow."

CHAPTER ELEVEN

"Thanks for such a wonderful evening," said Alison on the way home. "Including the entertainment. Bartholomew certainly knows how to grab the spotlight." She turned around to check on Joey in his car seat. The baby's eyes had started closing the minute Mike turned on the motor.

"Even Maggie and Thea were flummoxed. And all those excuses about helping pick out the perfect condo..." said Mike. "Just makes me laugh and, frankly, feel real good for him."

"Everything he said was true," added Paul, "about the condo. Who knows more about real estate than Bart? He'll negotiate well for her." He lowered his voice and stretched toward the front. "The little one's sound asleep. I think he's snoring."

"He had a great time," said Alison, "and the Parker children were wonderful with him. They had such patience singing "Baby Beluga" and all those other kiddie songs. Joey probably wore them out."

"He wore himself out! He's a perfect kid," said Mike. "You're a wonderful mom, doing a great job."

"Well, thanks. That's truly nice to hear, but I think you've contributed, too." Whether he was the male role model young boys needed or simply another adult paying attention to her son, Mike had definitely impressed Joey. The affection between them was genuine.

"Joey's a piece of cake, while Bart…I'm not sure," said Mike. "From what I understand, the woman's a tiger. Sounds like she won't need help with a thing."

"She's actually stunning," said Alison. "I met her only once, but I remember her well. It could be that after all these years, Bart Quinn has met his match."

"A *second* perfect match," said Mike, "with whom to share a life. Something to think about." His message couldn't have been clearer.

Paul coughed. "Son…"

"That's all I'm saying."

That's all he needed to say. Alison understood everything left unspoken. She had no problem with Bart's romance, no problem with second time around— for other people. She glanced at Mike behind the wheel. So handsome her blood raced, and she wanted to stroke his cheek. So kind and funny and reliable. She loved being with him. She had more fun with Mike around. Even with long work days—and they both had responsibilities elsewhere—she looked forward to reconnecting at night. She called it the "catching up conversation" with so much to talk about. Mike's evening visits topped off her days, like whipped cream on a cake.

But a lifetime commitment scared her. What if… What if…? Peter's image floated in her mind. Going down that road left her limp.

Mike pulled into his driveway and shut the engine. "I'll carry Joey."

"Great." Alison grabbed her purse and tote, said good night to Paul, and got out of the car.

Five minutes later, she and Mike were upstairs, tucking Joey into his big-boy bed, side rails attached. "He's definitely down for the night," said Mike.

"Just the way I like it." Leaving the door ajar, Alison shut the safety gate across the top of the stairs and led the way down toward the living room.

"A musical night?" Mike asked, glancing toward the cello.

She shook her head. He usually listened for an hour or so before sharing a hot drink and going home. "I'm taking a break, but you don't have to leave yet, do you?" Only nine o'clock—the evening still lay ahead, and the house felt too big, too empty. A wave of loneliness swept through her.

He clasped her hand and interwove their fingers. "I'm not going anywhere."

She tightened the hold, looked up at him, and whispered, "Will you kiss me?"

She'd barely uttered the request before his mouth was on hers. Like a spark to dried kindling, she ignited and burned as she hadn't in a long, long time. A strange feeling, but familiar and fantastic. She groaned.

His tongue invaded while they headed toward the couch. "You know where this is going, don't you?" he murmured between kisses. "If we don't stop…"

She knew where they were going, at least right then. His sports shirt didn't have a chance. One by one, she slipped each small white button through a slit. "Don't want to stop…"

Suddenly, she was in his arms, up in the air, until he laid her gently on the sofa cushions. "You are so beautiful…soft…" And then words weren't needed.

Her sweater disappeared, and she heard his breath catch. His shirt lay on the floor. Had she thrown it there?

Her bra was next, and when his fingers traced the outsides of her breasts, she gasped. And shivered. Her insides tightened; her legs stiffened. All happening so fast. Too fast.

"Oh, oh…this isn't going to—"

"Shh…" His tongue found her nipples. She held back a scream but managed to unbuckle his belt and pull.

"Easy, easy. I'm right here," he said in a raspy voice.

And he was. She rose higher to the beat of drums and the sound of trumpets, and he was with her, raising the tempo faster and faster until the final crescendo. She crashed hard. Could barely breathe. He sounded raspy, too. Until little by little, their gasps slowed down and returned to an even keel.

"That was the 1812—cannons and all," she whispered. "I'd almost forgotten what I've been missing."

Mike rose on his elbow. "But you're crying," he said in a horrified tone as he brushed tears away. "Did I hurt you?"

She stroked his cheek. "No, no. It's just that…it's like the first time…all over again. The discovery. It's fun and it's new…again."

"Thank God," he whispered. "You're incredible." He stroked her hair, cheek, and looked into her eyes. "I love you, Red. You know that, don't you?"

"I-I think I do. And I love you, too, Mike Romano. But I'm not too happy about it. I'm scared."

His kisses stopped further speech for a long time. Not that she minded the delay until he finally responded to her point.

"Everybody's scared of something."

She turned her head away. "Not like me. I don't want to jump in the deep end. I kind of like…what we have right now."

"And what would you call that?"

"Well…I guess it's a-a good friends-with-benefits arrangement."

"A…what?"

Uh-oh. Now *he* didn't look happy. "Hmm… a *special* friends-with-benefits arrangement."

His eyes glinted. "Just how special?"

"What do you mean? A mature relationship."

"Exclusive?"

"Of course!"

His laugh started small but continued to build until he was chortling and hugging her at the same time. "If it's tiny baby steps you want, then you'll get them. But honey, you're just fooling yourself! You've already left the shallow end way behind."

Maybe Mike was right. Maybe. But she couldn't expose herself to any more tragedy. No more risks. Dealing with more grief was simply too much to handle. On the other hand, a happy life beckoned. So tempting. She wanted it! Sighing with satisfaction at that admission, she realized she'd come a long way since moving into her house on Neptune Street. The thought of living like a hermit was scary enough to give her hives.

Joey slept later than usual the next day but was wide awake and dressed when his grandparents arrived mid-morning.

"Gamma, Gamma, Papa, Papa." He ran to them, arms up. And in her parents' faces, Alison saw hearts melt as they lifted him and passed him from one to the other. Kisses and joy abounded.

"Play wif me," ordered the boy. "Sing. Sing."

"Let's take our jackets off first," said David, suiting action to words.

Joey pulled his xylophone toward them in the front hall, squatted on the floor, and began playing and singing "Take Me Out to the Ball Game." Her parents joined in quietly. Alison saw, however, that they preferred listening only to Joey's attempt.

Her son didn't let them down. On pitch. Every note true. They'd work on his pronunciation in time.

"He's quite something," said her dad, a question in his voice.

Suddenly, Alison's maternal responsibilities took center stage. "You could say that, Dad. He's already led Beethoven's Fifth, kept a beat with Jason Parker on drums, and learned a dozen songs in an evening." She cleared her throat. "I've taken a good paying gig for a wedding in town, and the earnings are going toward a piano. A second-hand piano from the conservatory. Karen was appalled that I didn't have one, and now I think she was right. Joey needs a chance to explore music, and-and we'll see what happens."

Her folks looked from her to Joey. A big smile crossed her mom's face. "That's wonderful, Alison. And I don't mean the piano. You're back doing your own music, like when you played at the temple, and that's exactly where you belong. Sitting behind the cello."

"Mom and I will help you out with a piano," said her Dad. "How about fifty-fifty. Call it an early Christmaskuh gift. So, buy it. We're all set."

As Alison looked from her parents to her son, the connections fell into place. They wanted to see their daughter happy; she wanted her son happy. A desire passed from generation to generation. She felt tears behind her eyes. "So that's the way it works." She gestured from them to herself to Joey. A small circle.

"You bet."

A loud knock sounded, and a familiar voice called out, "Morning, folks," before the man walked in. One glance at Mike, and Alison felt the heat of a fiery blush suffuse her face.

"Good morning," she whispered.

He caressed her cheek but made his way to her parents. Shaking hands with her dad, a quick kiss on her mom's cheek. "So glad to see you again."

"And we, you," said Carol, glancing at her daughter.

"Mike, Mike, Mike." Joey ran over, and Mike hoisted him up high and settled him into his arms. "Did you tell Grandma and Papa where you were last night?"

A jumble of words and phrases spewed forth including, "Rest-a-ront. Mike likes clam chowder. Joey likes clam chowder. Yummy."

David's brow shot up. "Sounds like fun with a crowd. Interesting folks."

"The Lobster Pot's second to none in New England for food," said Mike. "And a great family place."

Carol looked from Alison to Mike and back to her daughter. "If you'd like to explore another more private venue tonight, we'll be happy to take care of Joey."

Her mom had great instincts. A chance for an ordinary date. No kids, no crowd, no noise or distractions. Just a chance for Ali and Mike to talk.

"What do you say, Ali?" Mike asked.

She met his questioning glance and nodded.

"Your folks are great." He turned his attention to the older couple. "Thanks very much. We don't get much baby-free time."

"Then we'll have to come down more often." Carol had the last word.

But Alison's thoughts flew to her in-laws. She hoped they'd want to visit, as well.

##

Alison hated to admit when Mike took his volunteer shift on Wednesdays, she had more time to practice without distractions. And the man was definitely a big distraction every day of the week. She smiled like a lunatic, and her heartbeat quickened just thinking about him. She often caught herself humming and staring into space. Her patience with Joey had become phenomenal, even when painting and cutting jack-o-lanterns the prior afternoon. Now the carved pumpkins sat on the front steps, where the chill autumn air would keep them whole until after Halloween.

Joey. If maternal love could grow, hers enveloped her entire being. Her precious son. Funny, delightful, clever, listening to the radio and humming pop songs even hours later. "Call Me Maybe" was a favorite. As was "Someone that I Used to Know." He had no idea what he was saying, but he kept the tune and beat even if he skipped a lot of words.

Playgroup, library, supermarket, errands. Every day was a new adventure, but that day had hit a new pinnacle. They'd taken the ferry to Boston, where she'd finally chosen a piano. Delivery was set for Friday.

After so many adventures, Joey had fallen asleep after dinner, and Alison wasted no time before sitting behind her cello. First up, the pieces for the concert and the wedding. Jason Parker had asked her to prepare one or two other appropriate songs in case the honored guests—the marathon victims—might need more time accessing the stage. Smetana's "The Moldau" had a beautiful lyrical melody with a strong beat for walking. A possible choice. Maybe the slow but deliberate "March of the Siamese Children" from *The King and I* would work. She'd do her very best for the honorees of this special event. Jason was so busy producing the concert, he needed no additional problems, especially from the soloist, who'd bring the honorees front and center stage.

Finally, she turned to her own work, the classical pieces that challenged her. The music that brought her joy. Much more than black dots on a page, the difference between the written notes and the realization of those notes was what it was all about. She and Ellen had talked about starting a small chamber group...if they could find a second violinist. Or a classical pianist. Ellen was working on a few of the same pieces Alison tackled.

Hours slipped by, and it was almost midnight by the time she lay her head on the pillow. Instant blackout. It seemed like mere seconds later, however, when a loud ringing dragged her up from the depths of sleep.

She thrust her arm toward the phone and groped for the receiver. "Hello...what—"

"It's Mike. Get up and out! Wrap the baby in a blanket and get out of the house. Do you understand me?"

"What? What?"

"There's a fire on our street. Get out. Now! We're on our way."

She dropped the phone, grabbed her bathrobe, and ran to the next room. "Okay, okay," she shouted.

"C'mon Joey." She hoisted him up, threw his blanket over the footed sleeper he wore, and ran down the stairs. Sweat covered her. Fear infused her. Nausea threatened. She thrust her feet into shoes she always left at the door. *Don't think. Just act.*

She'd locked up for the night, of course, and had to put Joey down to manipulate the latches. She heard barking on the other side. Then banging, and Paul's voice.

"Alison, Alison. Get up." He pounded on her door.

"I'm here." She finally got the door open and was almost mowed down by the big dog.

"C'mon, girl. Get across the street to my place. The fire's on this side. Close by."

Sirens blared and an ambulance pulled past. A louder blast filled the air as the next truck approached. Afraid to begin crossing, she waited. And there it was with lights flashing—tanks, hoses, ladders—and the volunteers. Mike! But all the firefighters were fully hidden by their helmets, uniforms, boots. Where was he? Her stomach tightened while her eyes strained to see more clearly.

Her worst nightmare come true. Another hero might fall. Just like Peter. *Please, God, not Michael Romano.* Goose bumps covered her skin, and she shivered, a whole-body shiver.

She thrust Joey at Paul and began running after the truck.

"No, Alison!" called Paul. "You'll be in the way. Come to my place."

She smelled a harsh odor, maybe burning rubber, and turned around. "I can stop him. I can't let him go in there." She pointed to the house two down from hers. Flames danced up the left side, close to the house next door.

"There's no one home. The Wilsons don't live here full-time," argued Paul.

But the firefighters still had to do their work. Walls could fall, roofs could collapse. She stepped forward.

"Guard her, Sophie." Mike's dad looked at her in apology. "I'm an old man, honey. I can't do it all."

The dog blocked her path. She took in the scene. Neighbors milled across the street, jackets over pajamas, house slippers on most. This time, her shiver came from the cold air. Reaching for Joey, she tucked his blanket more snugly around him and covered him with kisses. His eyes were wider than the wheels of the fire truck.

As they crossed to the opposite side of the street, Paul said, "Think how mad Bart will be, missing all the excitement."

Her laugh was sharp. "You've got him there." Paul probably wanted to distract her, but her eyes and mind followed the men on the red truck. Some held hoses trained on the flames; two others walked steadfastly inside.

She'd recognize his walk anywhere. One of those firefighters was Mike.

##

He hadn't had time to check on Alison, to see if she was outside in the crowd. He had to assume she was, that his dad's presence would calm her. This was not an adventure he would have chosen for her, but so be it. Real life happened, and his reality was the burning two-story, detached, wood-framed house near Alison's.

The "smells and bells" investigation was minimal. The fire was already established and easily visible by the time he arrived on the scene. He was on the Fast Attack team. First to enter the premises, search, and suppress the fire. His buddies would turn their hoses on the exterior walls.

With every sense alert, Mike entered the inferno. The walls were ablaze. Flames crackled and snapped, the noise a loud cacophony. Orange and red danced everywhere, hungry for more and moving with speed. He and his partner trained their hoses on the total scene—walls, ceiling, and floor ahead of them. Now the snaps and pops included the hiss of steam.

The fire had engulfed the kitchen and spread to the dining room. He anticipated total destruction of the house. Dang! One drenched wall started to rekindle. The fire must have smoldered for a long time before breaking through and being discovered. After all, how many people were out and about at midnight?

His eyes darted everywhere at once, which saved him from a piece of falling ceiling. Through the shimmering heat, he saw another piece fall. He kept moving. Thankfully, his personal compressed air supply saved his lungs from toxic inhalation. He and his partner worked in tandem for a short while before a third man joined them and motioned Mike outside.

"Next door is the new target."

Mike nodded and moved to his new assignment. Flames already licked the roof of the adjacent house, throwing shadows between the bright orange outbursts. A light breeze helped the fire grow. Too bad the only rain came from his hose. Where was the neighboring fire department? Pilgrim Cove trucks were the only ones at the site.

The crowd, much larger than when he'd arrived, watched and pointed. He knew their adrenaline was running high, too. But they stood too close to the incident. They needed crowd control. Like an answer to a prayer, over a bullhorn came the command to move back. A big man with a big German shepherd had taken charge. He walked the line, urging the crowd to back up. Good.

Finally another siren sounded in the near distance and became louder with every second. Mike sighed with relief. Their arrangement with nearby towns had worked after all. Too slowly, perhaps, but help had finally arrived.

Frowning at how swiftly the fire spread, he glanced toward Alison's house. Hers would go up next if they didn't contain the fire here. Her house and…her cello.

##

"Get that dog away from me. I have time, Paul. I have time to run across and get it."

"Mike would kill me, honey, if anything happened to you."

"You don't understand," she pleaded. "That cello's over three hundred years old. It's priceless! Not just the money but memories, history…"

She ran around Sophie. "It belonged to my teacher." Sobbing now at the lab's behavior, she placed Joey on the ground and made her pitch. "Sophie! Stay with the baby. Stay with Joey."

She eyed the dog, her house, and dashed across the street, up the porch steps, and slammed into a brick wall.

"Looking for this?"

In his gear, Mike was almost unrecognizable. Almost. She threw her arms around him. "You're safe. You're alive. I love you. I love you."

"I know," he said. "And I love you. But man, I shoulda been a hero sooner."

She froze, haunted again by a familiar refrain. Another hero had come along in her life, and she'd given him her heart. The irony threatened a sun shower of tears and laughter.

Shaking her head, she reached for the cello he held in his bare hand. "Can I get my bow?"

"No!" he roared. "Go back there. Stay with my dad. I have work to finish."

"Then put that glove back on," she ordered. "And be careful."

"Yes, ma'am."

CHAPTER TWELVE

"As soon as I turn my back, the town falls apart." Bart Quinn, in his role as president of Quinn Real Estate and Property Management, marched up and down the sidewalk two mornings after the fire, viewing the damages.

Alison, Mike, and Lila accompanied him as he barked out comments for his granddaughter to transcribe in her notebook. Lila mumbled about the chance of her granddad ever using a tape recorder and pushed a baby carriage. Joey walked alongside it, talking a mile a minute to the five-month-old infant but turning often to smile at his mom and Mike.

"The Wilsons and their insurers will get an official report," said Mike. "But I can tell you that the cause was electrical from frayed old wiring inside the walls. Couldn't handle all the new appliances they had. In fact, all these older homes should be rewired by a professional. The old wires can't handle the load."

"And I bet the breaker boxes don't shut off the current as they normally would because they never get the overload message." Bart tsked and shook his head.

"But at least no one was hurt and no arson was involved," said Lila. "Fewer problems for the town to deal with."

"True enough, lass."

Lila—partner in the business—winked at Alison before casting an innocent glance at Bart. "So was Honeybelle upset when you cut your visit short, Granddad?"

"She'll be back in Pilgrim Cove before long. Mark my words," said Bart.

"Well, of course," said Lila. "Thanksgiving and Christmas are coming and her family's here." Her voice resembled sweet honey, but the dancing light in her eyes revealed the truth.

"Family's part of it, but the woman's full of life. She's opening another art gallery down south. We were looking at locations. Imagine that. Two branches. Cape Cod and Florida."

What he omitted to add on after "imagine that" was *at her age*. Another gallery at her age. Alison squeezed Bart's arm with affection. "I think you've met your match, Bartholomew Quinn. She'll come home to Pilgrim Cove, and you'll never have a boring day with each other."

Lila, Bart, and Mike stopped walking, which brought Alison to a halt. Bart's quick chuckle was lined with glee. Mike clasped Alison's hand and pressed.

Lila spoke first. "Did you hear what you said, Ali? *Home* to Pilgrim Cove."

She had said it. And meant it. Raising her glance, she saw Mike's wide smile, the shine in his eyes.

"That word," he said with emphasis, "has a nice ring to it."

"I knew you'd be happy here, and want to make it permanent," boasted Bart.

"You bet she's happy." Mike's eyes adored her.

She inhaled a deep breath. "It-it could have been Joey and me in a burning house. And without Mike and his friends to put out the fire...who knows what else could have happened?" Her throat locked. Coughing, she managed to add, "In a small town, I think everyone looks out for everyone else... Heroes are born here, and even though there's TMI sometimes or even often, I guess it's worth the embarrassment of being everyone's business."

She stroked Joey's head, gave him a quick kiss. "Mike and I will figure out how to nurture him. As a growing boy first, and as a musician—if that's his calling—which I think it is." She laughed. "He reminds me...of me!"

She'd gotten Bart's attention. The man ignored the burned-out house. Ignored his granddaughter. And focused all his attention on Alison and Mike.

"Hoo-ha! Sea View House does it again!" He slapped his leg, clapped his hands. "The magic came with you, Alison Berg-Martin. You brought it with you to Neptune Street, and now you'll have to write your story in the journal." He raised his arms and took a small victory lap.

Lila shook her head and kissed the old man. "I don't know how you do it, Granddad, but you never fail."

Bart patted himself lightly in the stomach. "It's all in here, lassie, all in my gut about people. Ya either got it or you don't. And...I've got it!"

With laughter all around, Alison and Mike strolled to her house and left the others to finish their work.

"The piano is coming today," said Alison, "and my in-laws are visiting tomorrow and staying overnight. Join us for dinner after you finish at the store."

His brow lifted. "I'll stop by for a drink, and we'll see how it goes."

She squeezed his arm. "They think you saved us." Casting a glance at Joey, she added, "So it might be a bit easier than last time."

"They'll think I was just doing my job." He took her hands in his. "I'm not their son." The truth could not be refuted, but a frisson of hope colored his voice.

"I know that," she whispered. "But in my eyes, you are both men to be proud of. Men of honor."

His kiss held a promise that Alison responded to with full heart. And no guilt. She had enough love for everyone. She was not replacing Peter. She was making room in her heart for someone new to share her life.

##

Grandma Debra and Grandpa Robert arrived with flowers and candy. A huge bouquet for Alison, a large box of chocolate for Mike, and a backseat full of toys for Joey, including a small electronic keyboard. Quite a toy. They unloaded everything into the house.

"Two pianos!" Joey exclaimed. "One for Mommy and one for me."

Ali rolled her eyes. "From zero to two in one day!" She cuddled her son. "You can still play with me on the big one, too."

"Yes!" He ran to the room's center, twirled himself in circles, and did a summersault on the floor.

His grandparents beamed. "Perfect!" Debra turned to Ali. "He understands everything, and his speech has improved so much."

"I-I guess he's growing up, and he's been so busy with other children—some his own age and some older—musical friends. They seem to enjoy including him." Joey was the best bait she had to determine how interested the couple was in hearing about her current situation. She wanted harmony in her life as well as in her music.

"So this—this experiment of yours, moving here—is working out well?" asked Mrs. Martin.

She felt the blush, hated her fair skin for revealing her feelings so easily. "Yes, Debra, better than I expected. Better than I'd hoped."

A small silence settled over them. She started to speak, but Robert coughed at the same time and said, "We'd like to thank Mike Romano in person. A fire! When I think what could have happened. The wind blowing, the flames…" His face paled; the man looked haggard.

Alison ran to him and hugged tight. "But it didn't. Mike was on top of it, just like Peter would have been." *Peter.* She paused after saying his name…his holy name. But she couldn't hide forever. "Mike's a good guy, Robert. He's—become important to me. And to Joey."

Her father-in-law examined her first and then stared at his wife until her eyes met his. "It had to happen, Debra. She's young; she needs a good man at her side. And little Joey needs"—he gulped—"he needs one, too. To teach him…and show…him…how to grow from boy to man. He-he needs a dad."

Debra's eyes welled, and Alison seized her moment. Taking each of them by the arm, she voiced her prior thoughts because they made sense, at least to her.

"I'm not replacing Peter," she said. "That would be impossible. But I can make room in my heart for another man. And Joey will have two dads. One in Heaven and one right here with him on earth, right here in Pilgrim Cove." Her own tears flowed freely. The joy of finding another love brought with it a measure of pain.

"I believe they're both heroes," she whispered.

The couple stared at her and slowly nodded. "We-we'd like to know him better," said Robert. "For Joey's sake…and for yours, too."

Her heavy heart lightened. "And I'd love you to celebrate some other heroes with me the week before Christmas at TD Garden. The One Fund Boston concert, on behalf of the marathon victims. Will you come?"

"A symphony concert? Are you playing again?" Their confusion surprised her until she computed how few their phone conversations had been, and all centered on their grandson.

"Solo spot," she replied, hearing excitement infuse her voice. "But this time, it's rock, country, and whatever. Starring Jason Parker, Luis Torres…and some other big, big surprises."

"Wonderful!" Huge smiles, warm hugs, and congratulations followed. "Now we know you're truly getting back to yourself," said Robert. "We were worried. And we'd like to go, right, honey?"

Debra nodded. "We love Jason Parker's music. A real piano man." She began humming "At the Water's Edge," Jason's breakout song about Lila, his lost love. Lila at the water's edge. The Pilgrim Cove peninsula.

Her mother-in-law's voice held true. In the past, Alison had often complimented her and joked about Peter inheriting his lovely tenor from his mom. "It's nice to hear you singing again, Debra."

"I agree," added Robert, his quizzical expression lined with hope. "You sound great."

The woman stopped, a dazed look on her face. "I do, don't I?" Her surprise made Alison chuckle.

"More, Grandma. More." Joey waited patiently, his xylophone wand in hand. He'd been tapping out matching notes as Debra sang.

"Well, well, well." The woman's wide eyes reflected her amazement, and she knelt to the floor. "He's...playing...like he knows what he's doing."

"I think he does know, but I'm not worried anymore," said Alison. "He'll get all the encouragement he needs right here in Pilgrim Cove."

##

Butterfly wings danced inside Alison's stomach, providing the right amount of nervous energy she needed before a performance. In the car's front seat next to Mike, she sat quietly, focusing on the evening ahead. He'd insisted on driving her at the early reporting time. She could have gone alone as she so often had in Boston when playing with the South Shore Philharmonic. The regular season there had become a routine for travel with no choice to make between a thirty-minute ferry or a two-hour drive, the downside of winter in Pilgrim Cove.

"You're going to hit it out of the park," said Mike, reaching over and clasping her hand.

"Yes."

"The wedding you played at The Wayside Inn last month went off perfectly. Remember?"

"Yes."

"And you enjoyed it."

"Yes. Very much."

A chuckle followed. "Then...let's set a date."

"Yes... Wait. What did you say? A date?"

"Our own wedding date." He reached for her suddenly cold hand. "Sweetheart...it's time. And I promise, you won't have to provide the music."

His wink set her laughing. Laughing hard. She attributed it to nerves. "I do love you, Mike Romano. And I am ready to begin again. Somehow, I have confidence we'll figure everything out. Together."

146

"Children, careers, but most of all...you and me. Together."

As she looked at the strong man next to her, the man who loved her, teased her, challenged her, and brought flowers for her garden, her nervousness dissipated. "I *am* going to knock it out of the park tonight."

"In front of eighteen thousand, six hundred and twenty-four people. Sold out."

"Wow! That's a lot of people." About nine times the capacity of Symphony Hall and the other musical venues. "So, sooner or later?" she asked, her thoughts racing ahead.

"Sooner or later, what...?

"Our wedding. Sooner or later?"

"That's easy," he replied. "Sooner. Definitely sooner. As in, as soon as possible."

ASAP? "You mean Las Vegas?" she asked, giving it consideration.

He burst out laughing. "Nope. Don't want to alienate all of Pilgrim Cove. Especially my dad. So this is the first item on the figure-it-out list."

Just like they'd figure out the challenges that lay ahead. With Mike at her side, she'd be able to make decisions that worked for her and for them. She'd take her place back in the South Shore Philharmonic this year, and after that, who knew? She needed to make music to be happy. She needed Mike's love and little Joey to be happy. Maybe another child later on. In the end, she'd have everything she wanted, but maybe not all at the same time.

Man plans; God laughs. Ali shrugged.

Glancing at her love as he parked the car, she said, "No shadows anymore. I'm ready to begin again."

There must have been something in her voice. She heard his sharp inhale. Saw him yank the key from the ignition. And then he kissed her.

"I know you are, Red. Definitely worth the wait. You've made me the happiest man alive."

The house rocked. Starting with the national anthem, sung by over eighteen thousand people, the energy never wavered. As Jason Parker said at the mic, "The Boston Marathon is as American as baseball and apple pie. So in honor of our heroes, please rise." They stood and sang with one voice.

Alison waited backstage, listening, watching on a closed-circuit screen. Jason had put a fabulous band together, including some Boston musicians that she recognized. With the spotlight on him, Jason led from his place at the grand piano—standing, sitting, jumping, and having a great time. Major pop star Luis Torres brought the crowd to its feet. In the first half, the two men gave the audience what it wanted—hits, hits, and more hits, most written by Jason—and whetted their appetite for more. They interspersed slow with fast songs, and when they started Jason's signature piece, "At the Water's Edge," the Garden became quieter than a prayer.

That song was Alison's cue to make her way to the stage. And for the first time, she wondered if her one little cello could command a venue as large as the TD Garden. She sat partly upstage, a third of the way across, so the guests had room to be front and center.

The house lights brightened but not starkly. Jason introduced the mayor of Boston, who would present ten guests of honor, representing the 260 hurt in the blast, many of whom were in attendance that night. Four people had been slain. Two people lost double limbs, and fourteen lost single limbs—including Rebecca Hart Fielding of Pilgrim Cove.

Jason approached her at a fast pace. "Listen up, kiddo. A slight change. After you begin playing, you'll hear a familiar voice singing with you. Mariah Carey is in the house and backstage. It's her song. So have at it. And have fun."

What? Did he say the singer was here? She sat straighter. She was a pro, wasn't she? "No problem." Forget "Chariots of Fire" and every other piece she'd prepared. It was "Hero" all the way. She looked at the first honoree, nodded, began to play, and sensed someone walking behind her. Then heard the voice. And the growing applause of recognition.

Alison had practiced the music so often she could perform it by heart. Which she did in order to follow the singer as she graciously approached each hero, paused, and sang only to that one person. Each one a hero. A wonderful, thoughtful gesture.

Many heroes had come along that night. All survivors in heart, mind, and spirit. Including...her!

With that startling discovery, a smile grew slowly across Alison's face. Her eyes, however, remained glued to the singer.

They ended together in perfect harmony, with Ms. Carey standing next to Alison. Making eye contact, they grinned, enjoying the shared moment. "Thanks," said the singer. "You are a beautiful musician, and that is one beautiful instrument."

"Are we going to march them off after they speak?" whispered Ali.

"Not sure. The Boss is here. He might do "Born to Run." You know—marathon and all."

"But I don't know it," said Alison, worried. She listened to pop casually but didn't spend time playing it.

The woman laughed. "He won't need you."

They remained quiet as the first guest began talking. Alison saw Rebecca center stage. "Watch my friend over there," she whispered, "the one in the red sweater. A little birdie told me she had something special going on."

Five minutes later, Rebecca began speaking. Alison didn't know exactly what to expect. The woman stood tall, her long dark hair hanging loosely below her shoulders. She'd matched the red sweater with a flared black skirt, and her first words into the mic attached to that sweater were: "Don't call me a victim."

Her voice came through loud and strong. The audience leaned in.

"I was at the wrong place at the wrong time. So it was bad luck. Don't call me a victim"—she paused—"except if you understand that victims fight back. Your donations to One Fund Boston make our fight possible. First it's the physical and then it's the mental."

She paced a few steps back and forth. "I lost one leg above my knee. But instead of speaking a thousand words, let me show you a picture."

As Alison watched, Rebecca unbuttoned her skirt and let it fall to the floor. She wore short shorts and two inch heels. She posed, one hand on her hip, the other behind her head. Whistles and cat calls came from the audience as she walked back and forth and in a circle.

"Which leg did I lose?" she challenged.

More applause. She held up her hand and waited for quiet. "There's one more thing you should know. The most important thing. After the bombing, I met a wonderful man. I fell madly in love and got married." She put her hand up to shade her eyes. "And my darling is in the house somewhere. Where are you, Adam?"

Alison watched, mesmerized. What was Rebecca thinking? What was she doing?

"Your friend sure knows how to grab attention," whispered Mariah.

"I've never seen her like this before."

Rebecca began speaking again, and Alison listened hard.

"Oh, there you are, Adam. I have such good news that I saved it for tonight, because…it just seemed right. We all need good news sometimes." She looked at the audience. "Don't we?"

They were behind her a hundred percent.

"What's going on, Rebecca?" Adam's voice boomed through his handheld mic as he now stood next to his wife. Alison guessed the eighteen thousand other people didn't exist for him at that moment.

"We're—we're having a baby!" She looked from Adam to the audience, extended her arm, and waved it graciously from left to right. "So, my friends, when you remember tonight, when you think of the victims, remember that with a little help, we fight back. And on a personal note, also remember that this *victim* has never been happier."

The crowd roared and cheered. Rebecca cried. Adam hugged his wife, and Jason ran over to the couple.

"Your friend's making headlines tomorrow," said Mariah Carey. "Star billing."

"But that's good, isn't it?" asked Alison. "This is a fundraiser, and she's proof that a little help can go a long way."

"Let's play them off," said the singer. "Springsteen isn't…

And then they heard the gravelly voice…with the energy and dynamic to tear the house down.

"It seems to me," said Alison, rising from her chair, "that Jason Parker has produced one heck of a hit show. Lots of fun and full of good surprises."

CHAPTER THIRTEEN

Bart Quinn had never thought of himself as a ladies' man. He was a family man, businessman, and a proud citizen of Pilgrim Cove. He knew his town and the town knew him. Until…Honeybelle showed up.

On the morning after the concert, he walked down the Sea View House driveway, bagels in hand, and let himself into the kitchen. Honey met him at the door, a wide smile in greeting and the tang of sizzling garlic following her, the promise of dinner to come.

With Joy MacKenzie and Logan Nash away on their honeymoon, he and Honey had been in charge for the week, taking care of their little Bonnie, who'd become Honey's great-niece. And, of course, Ajax, the shepherd, back from the Mid East with Logan. Honey insisted the war dog thought *he* was in charge. Bart had to admit Ajax guarded them as though they were babies. Not necessary in Pilgrim Cove, but…tell that to a dog.

"We'll have a big crowd here this afternoon, Honey. Why are you fussing with all the cooking? My girls can cater from the Lobster Pot."

"I'm cooking because I like to cook! So settle down, worrywart. And give me those bagels before you slice open your hand."

"Bossy, bossy." But his heart turned over. The spunky woman with the twinkling blue eyes and dangling earrings had him coming and going. The world seemed a brighter place when he hadn't realized his vision had dulled since...since he'd lost Rosemary.

Sea View House had never looked better. With Christmas only a few days away, the current tenants had made it a home. Joy had decorated the mantel and tree before going on her honeymoon, and if the creative kindergarten teacher had left corners untouched, Mike Romano had sent over enough poinsettias to fill them.

"When is three o'clock, Auntie Honey?" Little Bonnie looked up from the floor where she was working on her latest art project.

"In just a few more hours, baby. Your new mommy and daddy will walk through that door and—"

"Everyone will be together and Grandma Marie, too."

Bart pulled up a chair next to the child. "It's a party, lass. The whole town will be here to celebrate all good things."

He felt a soft hand on his shoulder. "Everywhere you go is a party, Bart Quinn. And you know it."

He rose and hugged the woman, his grin so wide it hurt. "Then why are you running back to Florida after the holidays? You're a born and bred New Englander!"

"But I also love sunshine. And I've got a business to open. Do you know how many customers of mine spend their winters down south? I'd be crazy not to expand the gallery. The slush and snow will no longer be on my radar. And good riddance."

Except for Bonnie's humming, quiet set in. An unsettled quiet. "You'll miss me," said Bart, his heart thumping, hoping to see the truth of his words reflect in her eyes.

She inclined her head. "You helped me buy my new place. You know there's room for…special guests."

Is that how she thought of him? Did he, a man of many years, and after more than a decade alone, still need the admiration of a particular lady? Or was it a *want*?

Oh, yeah. He began to chuckle. That's it. What man didn't want to be viewed as special? Now he relaxed. Honesty. That's what drove his gut feelings.

As for Honey's condo, it had space, and he'd driven a good price. Or maybe she'd let him. The woman was no slouch in business. But for him to leave Pilgrim Cove? That was another question. He had a business, too. And Sea View House…and all his friends.

"Ach…my head's splitting." So unlike him to postpone a discussion with a feeble excuse.

"You're heart's splitting, not your head." Honey walked to the stove and began stirring sauce.

Maybe so. Maybe so.

##

By three o'clock, Sea View House was bursting with Bart's friends, family, and some of the younger folks he'd chosen as the home's tenants in recent years. Rebecca Hart. Logan Nash. Joy MacKenzie. Alison Berg-Martin. They'd all met their match…both in him and through him. His own precious Lila included. His beautiful granddaughter with smarts and strength he'd like to take credit for. But all he'd done was provide her opportunity to grow.

She and Jason…perfect together. And the gal was a perfect business partner for Bart, shaking him up with her computers but keeping the office updated and competitive. More important, his Lila knew almost as much as he did about the town—every square block including what lay beneath the streets!

Today, however, Rebecca Fielding was the talk of Pilgrim Cove. Rebecca and Adam, who'd stopped the show last night. And of course, Adam's ten-year-old daughter, Sara, who now had a new mom and would soon be a big sister. The way it should be. A beautiful family.

"Counting the notches on that wedding belt?" asked Lou Goodman, handing Bart a glass of champagne.

"That I am, Louis. Look around. In just this year, we'll have had two weddings with a third coming up."

"Granted, it's a special place," said Lou. "For Pearl and me, too. With our Rachel living in this house awhile ago and meeting Jack…" His words trailed off. "Lots of memories and a happy day for all of us." He slapped Bart's shoulder. "I'll give you full credit for your instincts, old friend. They worked."

But if he were gone…left town…who…?

All his ROMEO buddies—Lou and Pearl, Max and Marsha Rosen, Rick and Dee O'Brien, Sam Parker, Joe Cavelli, Ralph Bigelow—were all still living, volunteering, and playing cards here. But none were him!

His gaze focused on Honey. The woman's friendly cheer enhanced her sparkle as she visited with each guest.

"Your Honey is another one," said Lou, "who's never met a stranger. She's so like you in that way."

"I agree," said his wife. "Look at her making the rounds with folks she barely knows. She's a nice lady, Bartholomew."

Bart glanced from one to the other. "Ach…I know, I know."

The couple smiled at each other. "As long as you do, we're content."

They left him just as Lila approached. "Jason's still sleeping, but he'll be here in a bit. What a night!"

"Aye, it was. Raised lots of money, too."

"Jason steps up when he's needed. He's never let me down since he—let's say, since he fought his demons, became a man, and returned here."

Bart patted her hands. "He adores you, lassie. You know that. And with your precious Katie and now Baby Rosemary, you've got it all."

"But it was you, Granddad! You came to my rescue way back when. Thank you for that. For letting me have space from Mom and live with you."

She kissed him on the cheek, and his heart overflowed. He felt the love, yes, but also heard something else. Her voice sounded poignant, wistful. Like a good-bye. "What is it, lassie?"

Lila smiled and nodded toward Honeybelle. "I like her, Granddad. And I love you. Don't be afraid to try like I was. Let Sea View House work its magic. I say, go for it!"

He just might surprise them.

"Oh, here's Jason and the Romano men with Alison and little Joey." And she was off to greet them.

Bartholomew Quinn stood tall, gazed from one chatting group to another, took a deep breath, and raised his glass. "My dear friends," he began, "I have something to say. And you'll want to have a glass of champagne nearby."

"Shush, shush...Bart's talking."

He didn't let them see his grin. Honestly, he loved being the center of attention. But he didn't grab it without reason.

"You've heard me say many times," he began, "that Pilgrim Cove was just a six-mile finger in the ocean. A spit of peninsula that no one's heard of."

Nods and chuckles all around.

"But we are much more than that." He paused while folks settled down again. "In this place we call home, our friends rally round us when times are hard. We're never alone even if we think we want to be." He glanced at Alison.

"We celebrate the good times, and who doesn't love a party? But most of all, in this place we call home, we poke our noses into each other's business!"

He waited for the brief laughter to fade. "We are also part of the larger world, and never forget that. Look at last night. That was special, and our folks were smack dab in the middle of it! That's Pilgrim Cove, too."

Jason and Lila held hands. Rebecca and Adam, also. Mike Romano kissed Alison on the mouth. Ooh…nice.

"There are many small towns along the Atlantic coast, but there is only one Pilgrim Cove. And one Sea View House. I salute the ROMEOs, my friends who helped me establish the Sea View House Foundation and maintain the building. Without the ROMEOs, the project would never have come to fruition." He raised his glass high and sipped. Others applauded.

"When I look around this room, I see young people who've been touched by the magic, house, and the town. In fact, they now call Pilgrim Cove home. I salute each of you. But I'm taking some credit for keeping you here!" Another sip.

"Patience, my friends. Just one more acknowledgement. An important one—to me." He looked toward Honey and raised his glass. "If you haven't already met the lass, I'd like for you to meet a special friend of mine, Ms. Honeybelle

MacKenzie. She…ah…makes me very happy. And she is now living in Sea View House!"

"So you all know what that means," called out Lila, beaming at the assembly.

"I'm here only until I leave for Florida," said Honey, standing next to Bart.

"So here's the unvarnished, no-Blarney-Stone truth," said Bart. "I need you all. Lads and lasses. I know I can count on you while I take a little winter vacation…a few months to explore…"

"Quit while you're ahead," murmured Honey, giving him a tight hug.

More whistles, more applause. And lots of slaps on the back.

Bart took it all in. His wonderful friends, the young couples, their children now and those yet to be born. A renewal from generation to generation.

He wasn't worried anymore. Pilgrim Cove was in good hands. Sea View House, too. As for the power of the place? Was it love or magic? He'd let others argue the point. As for him, a second-chance love was magic enough.

SEA VIEW HOUSE JOURNAL

(Pilgrim Cove Series)

From Laura McCloud Parker—I arrived at Sea View House in March, looking for a place to catch my breath and get on with life. I'd just lost my mom and completed my own breast cancer treatment, one event right after the other. The first person I met in Pilgrim Cove, besides Bart Quinn, was Matt Parker. And the first part of him I saw was his jeans and work boots, sticking out from beneath my kitchen sink. "Hand me the wrench," he said, thinking I was his son. How could I have known then that living in this *House on the Beach* would forever change my life? Bart says it's a magical place. I'm not arguing.....

From Shelley Anderson Stone—The children and I arrived at Sea View House on Memorial Day weekend. Divorce hurts everybody, and we all needed time to recover. Bart Quinn had given us the large apartment downstairs called the Captain's Quarters. I had no idea that Daniel Stone would be living upstairs in the Crow's Nest, dealing with his own grief. I also had no idea he would rock my world—in the very best of ways—and that we'd provide each other with a second chance at love. Looking back, I can say that season was *No Ordinary Summer* for any of us....

From Daniel Stone—Read Shelley's account. Here's my P.S.: If there's any magic at all, it was provided by Jesse, my golden retriever. Two little kids and a golden? Pure magic.

From Rachel Goodman Levine—Like a prodigal daughter, I returned to my hometown of Pilgrim Cove in the fall, trying to prove myself as an assistant principal of the high school. Instead of living with my folks, I landed at Sea View House. I wasn't alone there. Thank you, Bart Quinn! Marine biologist Jack Levine had settled into the Crow's Nest. My initial delight turned to dismay when Jack joined my teaching staff, breaking all the rules with his unorthodox methods. And getting me into trouble. It was then the magic happened. The discovery. The love. Somehow, we *Reluctant Housemates* are now housemates forever right here in Pilgrim Cove....

From Jack Levine—Read Rachel's story. All I'll say is: magic, my eye! Sure, I'll admit that sailors are a superstitious bunch. But here's what really happened: My boat went missing and shook her up. It wasn't magic. It was a miracle! All of it. So believe what you want.

From Jason Parker—I came back after nine years because I couldn't outrun the pain. Prom night. A car wreck. My twin brother gone. Our music gone with him. Except not. I've got platinum behind me, and what does it mean? Nothing without the folks I love. Less than nothing without Lila Sullivan. She's always been the one, the only one for me. Bless Bart Quinn for lending me Sea View House. My daughter was conceived there a long time ago. But I didn't know anything about her all those years. Folks might call Katie *The Daughter He Never Knew*, and they'd be right. But I know her now. As for her mom and me…? Sea View House came through for us again. Our wedding took place right there. I believe in the magic. I believe in happily ever after. If that's not love, what is?

From Lila Sullivan Parker—Read Jason's account. All I'll add is that the right girl for lovely Adam Fielding is still out there. Jason's return saved Adam and me from a tepid marriage of convenience. We both deserved more. My money's on Adam and Sea View House.

(Sea View House Series)

From Rebecca Hart Fielding—It's summer again, a year since the last entry in this journal. The magic is still here. In this place, in this town, in its people. After the Boston Marathon, I arrived at Sea View House with no expectations except to focus on rehab. I wanted to hide, but that's impossible in Pilgrim Cove. In a nutshell, I met Adam in a bar. A nice bar at The Wayside Inn. It was definitely *not* love at first sight. But something changed along the way.

From Adam Fielding—We fell in love. That's what happened. That's the magic everyone talks about. No woo-woo. No smoke and mirrors. Scientists don't believe in that stuff. When Becca came to Sea View House, all she wanted to do was walk again. She was stubborn. She was proud. And she was determined to remain the athlete she'd always been. I'm happy to say that ***Her Long Walk Home*** brought her straight into my arms.

From Joy MacKenzie Nash – If anyone needed the magic of Sea View House, it was Logan and me. He didn't believe in it, of course. But grief lived in my heart, and I was open to anything. How ironic that this kindergarten teacher couldn't have her own children. I pretended to be happy. Maybe I overdid the act. When Logan met me, he thought I was a ditz, and I thought he was the loneliest person I'd ever met, always hiding behind his camera.

From Logan Nash – Love stared at me through the lens of my Nikon. Joy, Joy, Joy. She was everywhere. But what I did I know about love? Nothing. I was a foster care kid, never dreaming of a family of my own, not even knowing how an ordinary family worked. And the magic? When Joy said yes, her eyes shining with love, I knew that between us, she'd get ***Her Picture-Perfect Family***. And so would I. That's magic enough for me.

From Alison Berg-Romano – After my husband died, I wasn't looking for another love or another hero. The grief and guilt following his death haunted me. All I wanted was a safe, quiet life, a private life away from the city. I took my infant son, and rented a house in cozy Pilgrim Cove. Little did I know Mike Romano lived across the street. Mike didn't believe in quiet. Or solitude. Or privacy. He drove me crazy until I saw the truth. He was my cheering section. My go-to guy. He had my back. And his eyes shone with love when he looked my way. But not even for me, would he stop fighting fires in Pilgrim Cove.

From Mike Romano – Starting over is not easy, but Ali is much stronger than she thinks. All I did was nag and tease and challenge her—and play with baby Joey—until she finally agreed to a dinner date. I'm sure she just wanted to shut me up and live her quiet life again. But I couldn't let that happen. She's too brave, beautiful and talented to give up on life. In her, I saw myself, no stranger to second chances. Her husband was a hero, and I'm certainly not qualified as **Her Second-Chance Hero**. I'm just a guy giving back to the town I love. And to the woman who stole my heart.

From Bartholomew Quinn – *It's all about the magic.* That's the truth, but these young people refuse to admit it. So let's be scientific. What do these loving couples have in common? **Sea View House!** So is it mere coincidence that in recent times seven couples met there, fell in love, and got married afterwards? No! It's *not* coincidence. The seaside location with all the sun and sand might provide the perfect atmosphere, but in the end, it's magic.

Sea View House has been an enchanted hideaway from the beginning, because that's what grieving folks need. A special place to heal. I expect the healing powers of Sea View House will continue long after I'm gone. But to tell the truth, I've got no plans to go anywhere yet…except to Florida for a little while. With a gal who-who likes my company. A gal who made this old heart race like a young stallion's. But I can also see that

Honeybelle's eyes gleam when I look her way. It seems the Sea View House charm is not only for the young, but for the young-at-heart, too. Did I mention that Honeybelle MacKenzie happens to live there at the moment?

Imagine! After all this time, the magic's come around to touch me!

HELLO FROM LINDA

Dear Reader,

Thank you for choosing to read ***Her Second-Chance Hero***. I hope the story kept you turning the pages as Alison Berg-Martin and Mike Romano figured out how wonderful second chances are for those with courage and open hearts.

I also hope you enjoyed your visit to Pilgrim Cove and the entire *Sea View House* trilogy. If this story introduced you to the cozy beach town, I hope you will purchase the first two books so you can catch up! ***Her Long Walk Home*** and ***Her Picture-Perfect Family***.

If you enjoyed ***Her Second-Chance Hero***, I would truly appreciate your help in getting the word out by writing a review and posting it wherever you bought the book or on Goodreads. Short is good! A sentence or two about how the book made you feel is perfect. You have my deep thanks for your time and effort.

Be the first to know about my new writing projects and book releases, by visiting my website: *www.linda-barrett.com* and signing up for my newsletter here:

http://lindabarrett.authornewsletters.com/?p=subscribe &id=3. You'll receive a free gift if you do! You can also keep up with me on
Facebook: *www.facebook.com/linda.barrett.353*

I'm very grateful for your help in getting the word out about **Her Second-Chance Hero** and the entire *Sea View House* trilogy. If you're looking for another emotional Linda Barrett read, my other novels are listed here and are available electronically and in print.

With many thanks,
Linda

P.S. If you like blending laughter and tears, try **The Soldier and the Rose**, a love story from the Greatest Generation. Two soldiers go off to war in Europe. Both from Brooklyn, NY. Only one returns home. Who is Rose's true love? The man she married with all her heart? Or the man who married her with all of his?

LINDA BARRETT BOOKS

NOVELS—ROMANCE:

(Sea View House Series)
Her Long Walk Home, 2015 (Bk. 1)
Her Picture-Perfect Family, 2015 (Bk. 2)
Her Second-Chance Hero, 2016 (Bk. 3)

(Harlequin Books, Superromance)
Quarterback Daddy, 2010
Summer at the Lake, 2009
Houseful of Strangers, 2007
A Man of Honor, 2006

(Pilgrim Cove Series - Harlequin Books)
The House on the Beach, 2004 (Bk. 1)
No Ordinary Summer, 2004 (Bk. 2)
Reluctant Housemates, 2005 (Bk. 3)
The Daughter He Never Knew, 2005 (Bk. 4)

The Inn at Oak Creek, 2003
The Apple Orchard, 2002
True-Blue Texan, 2001
Love, Money and Amanda Shaw, 2001

NOVELS—WOMEN'S FICTION:

The Soldier and the Rose, 2014
Family Interrupted, 2013

SHORT NOVELLA:

Man of the House, 2013 (part of *Celebrate Romance* anthology with four other authors)

MEMOIR:

HOPEFULLY EVER AFTER: Breast Cancer, Life and Me, 2013 (true story about surviving breast cancer twice)

Printed in Great Britain
by Amazon